D1254147

Other Books Translated by Neil Bermel

The Widow Killer by Pavel Kohout

I Am Snowing by Pavel Kohout

Fingers Pointing Somewhere Else

Stories by

Daniela Fischerová

Translated from the Czech by

Neil Bermel

Catbird Press
A Garrigue Book

Originally published in Czech as *Prst, který se nikdy nedotkne*

First English-language edition.

CATBIRD PRESS
16 Windsor Road, North Haven, CT 06473
800-360-2391; catbird@pipeline.com; www.catbirdpress.com
Our books are distributed by
Independent Publishers Group

Library of Congress Cataloging-in-Publication
Fischerová, Daniela.
[Prst, který se nikdy nedotkne. English]
Fingers pointing somewhere else / by Daniela Fischerová ;
translated from the Czech by Neil Bermel. -- 1st English-language ed.
"Garrigue book."
ISBN 0-945774-44-3 (cloth : alk. paper)
1. Fischerová, Daniela. Translations into English. I. Bermel, Neil. II. Title.
PG5039.16.I82P7713 2000
891.8'636--dc21 99-16409 CIP

Contents

Czech Pronunciation Guide

b, d, f, m, n, s, t, v, z - like in English
c - like ts in oats
č - like ch in child
ch - one letter; something like ch in loch
d' - soft, like d in duty (see ě below)
g - always hard
h - like h in have, but more open
j - like y in you
l - like l in leave
ň - like n in new (see ě below)
p - like our p, but without aspiration
r - rolled
ř - pronounce r with tip of tongue vibrating against upper teeth, usually approximated by English speakers by combining r with s in pleasure
š - like sh in ship
t' - soft, like t in tuesday (see ě below)
ž - like s in pleasure

a - like u in cup, but more open
á - hold it longer
e - like e in set, but more open
é - hold it longer
ě - after b, m, n, p: usually approximated by English speakers by saying the consonant plus yeah; after d and t, soften the consonant by placing tongue at tip of upper teeth
i, y - like i in sit, but more closed
í, ý - hold it longer, like ea in seat
o - like o in not, but less open
ó - hold it longer, like aw in lawn
u - like oo in book
ú, ů - hold it longer, like oo in stool
ou, au, and eu are Czech dipthongs

Rule No. 1 - Always place accent on the first syllable of a word.
Rule No. 2 - Pronounce all letters.

Translator's Preface

In the final story of this collection, Fischerová puts her finger on a problem all translators face. At one point, an old man stares critically at his young but decrepit nephew and thinks: "How old he looks! At thirty-one I looked my thirty-one years, but I aged differently. There was a powerful current of youth, and a powerful current of old age surging against it, and their waters mixed with a roar, like a dam bursting. But him — he's a ditch full of dried-up mud."

The narrator follows this interior monologue with the comment: "He saw this image with absolute clarity, but he did not think it, and if he had had to describe his nephew's aging, he would not have found the word *water,* nor the word *ditch,* nor the word *current.*"

All translators struggle with this need to look behind the words, to return to the essential images that underlie them. And yet, a piece of literature doesn't reduce to a collection of pictures, sounds, smells, flavors. A literary translation's success hangs on the goals and compromises the translator adopts when working with the author's prose, trying to balance these two ways of perceiving the text.

Authors like Daniela Fischerová, who chooses her words with extraordinary care, tempt the translator to bend all his effort to literal meaning. Fischerová's prose constantly surprises in the way it combines unusual images and situates words in unexpected proximity to each other, keeping the reader slightly off balance, attentive to the linguistic medium as well as the literary message. This sense of unsteadiness and heightened awareness is central to the experience of reading Fischerová in Czech — but it is not all there is to it.

In the end, translating the literal meaning of a sentence is straightforward. The agonizing, frustrating, hair-pulling bit is reducing the first draft to something readable that mirrors not only the author's meaning but also her style and impact. Fischerová's language is deceptively simple and compact. She has told me that she is as proud of what is *not* in these stories as of what is. Every word is there on purpose; all superfluities have been stripped away. Can a translator ignore this sort of mandate? A translation that fails to account for the economy and sound of the original will give the reader a radically different — and probably markedly inferior — experience.

At each juncture, then, I have tried to recreate in English this balance between sense and style. This is where, I suspect, I am a bit obsessive. Right now, as I finish up the translation, I frequently count words and syllables on my fingers, asking myself if, for instance, I can really justify having twelve words where Fischerová gets away with only eight. I also scan the meter, read aloud, and measure the text visually, flipping back and forth between the original and the translation, trying to see whether the aural and visual impact of the two texts is roughly parallel. These are all primitive tools, but the translator needs some defenses against verbosity.

As you may have gathered, what I hope you won't find here is one of those zealously "faithful" translations that give you the feeling you're reading something in an unfamiliar language, but with English words. I have no interest in such translations, either as a reader or as a translator. They serve no one outside the academy, and as I am also a teacher of Czech, I propose that those occasional academicians who want to study Czech literature in gory detail make the effort to learn the language. We could use the business, anyway.

Here are a few of the balancing acts I've done in this translation.

Fischerová constantly twists clichés and proverbs to fit her themes, a tactic that inevitably puts the translator on the rack. In "Letter for President Eisenhower," the narrator, a young girl, writes about her first essay, "A Merry Christmas Party," which she says was *vycucaná z prstu*, 'made up.' She then goes on to say that *vycucaným dětem se v ní dějí vycucané věci,* literally 'in it, made-up things happen to made-up children.' The problem is that the expression *vycucaný z prstu* literally means 'sucked from one's finger,' echoing the 'finger pointing somewhere else,' Fischerová's image for fiction and storytelling. The children and events are literally 'sucked out,' not 'made up.' This image will not survive in English, but I resisted using the pedestrian *made-up*. Instead, I substituted another metaphor: *My "Merry Christmas Party" was made up out of thin air. About thin-air kids doing thin-air things.* In this resolution, the unusualness of the combinations (*thin-air kids, thin-air things*) mirrors the effect in the Czech. Although the original allusion is lost, *thin air* becomes a forward reference to later in the story, when the narrator writes a scenario about mountain climbing. So the reference to creativity survives, if in an attenuated form.

In other places, I simply let the author's words stand, even though I knew their impact would be diluted by their cultural journey. For instance, in the story "Dhum," a doctor describes his fascination with women who are "as bitterly beautiful and neglected as an October grave." *An October grave?* In Czech culture, All Souls' Eve falls in the first week of November; after nightfall, people visit the resting places of their deceased friends and family to light candles in their memory. On the days leading up to it, the cemeteries are crowded with people brushing the gravesites free of leaves, pulling weeds and cleaning the stones, preparing for the holiday. But by the following October many of the graves are overgrown and desolate once again. Without this cultural context, half the impact of the simile is lost. But the image of a grave in cold autumn is still striking enough, I felt, to survive the transition.

Sometimes, however, respecting the original is of dubious value to the English-language reader. Czech, like many European languages, distinguishes between a formal and informal *you* (respectively *vy* and *ty*). The use of one or another conveys a wealth of information about a relationship. As might be expected from a writer so interested in language, Fischerová remarks on this distinction at points. When speaking of a friend in the story "Far and Near," the narrator says, "we never stopped saying *vy* to each other." And when two characters speak English in the story "Dhum," the narrator notes that the Czech one "subconsciously translated the English *you* as *vy*." Here, as a translator, I simply throw up my hands. Footnoting the sentence and explaining it exhaustively would solve one problem while instantly creating another. The Czech sentence explains matters economically in five words, not fifty. It does not distract the reader from the flow of the text nor introduce a new and unfamiliar concept. So I let such instances lie. In the first case, I translated it as *we never dropped the formalities,* while in the second I left it out altogether. And as for the rest of the *ty-vy* relationships in this book, interesting or no, they go unremarked and unmentioned in the translation.

*

A translator, talented or otherwise, is only as good as those who back him up. So there are a few people waiting for their due.

For a non-native speaker of Czech like myself, every text has dark corners that no dictionary or handbook can illuminate. A native-speaker consultant is an absolute must — but as every translator quickly learns, very few people have the breadth of knowledge and the grasp of translators' issues to give reliable, solid advice. I am lucky to have a very kind, patient and extraordinarily knowledgeable consultant in Prague, Ilona Kořánová. Herself an experienced translator from English who has worked with fiction, films, and television, she has over the past seven years fielded hundreds of questions from me about obscure words, quotations, idioms, names, customs and slang words. There is many a phrase in these stories that we have puzzled through over coffee or discussed at length by e-mail, and if this book reads by and large smoothly, I have Ilona to thank for the lack of "speed bumps" in it.

I also owe a debt to Dr. Miriam Jelinek, School of East Asian Studies, and Dr. Petr Kopecký, Department of Politics, both of Sheffield University, and to Dr. Ivana Bozděchová of the Czech Language Department at Charles University, for their helpful and insightful commentary. Andrew Swartz was the first to wade into the English version with no recourse to the Czech, and offered many valuable comments. My father, Albert Bermel, himself a translator (of French and Italian drama), deserves thanks for his advice and support over the years. I would be remiss in not mentioning Catbird Press, in the person of Robert Wechsler, for taking my work from rough draft to final version with great care and insight, and for initiating numerous provocative and interesting discussions along the way.

*

There are two ways to translate words from a language far removed in time, Fischerová says in this volume's final story. "One is with the eternal present's abbreviated arc, in the belief that the sense of words and things endures and, like Zeno's arrow, hangs in flight. The other keeps to Babel's model, clinging anxiously to the literal meaning of individual words confined to the solitary cell of their place and time. We choose the first method, but this does not mean it is the better one."

The dilemma, of course, applies to all languages, and every translator is intimately familiar with it. I've striven to do justice to Fischerová's work in Zenoic fashion: if I've succeeded, the arrow will remain suspended, and the stories will seize you and engage you, as good works of fiction should, while the gears and machinery of my translation remain essentially invisible. Happy reading.

Neil Bermel
Sheffield, England
August 1999

My Conversations with Aunt Marie

Is love finite or eternal? Aha!

I am not quite five. A hazy memory: my parents have arrived on the evening train. Look: Mother had her braids cut off. Do I like it? I don't. On the way back, Grandma cries over the braids. Then mother too bursts into tears. On a balcony in the twilight I study the curls almost oozing from her head — but I don't remember that house having a balcony.

Another memory: at a bend in the fence, tiny lavender flowers called slipperwort. I stick my fingers into them. I am sent to the garden for parsley, but return with empty hands (what is "parsley"?). My father the musician, who my grandma respectfully asks to write down the music for the song I "composed" yesterday. We are all standing downstairs in the hallway (Father has just arrived), each of them is singing over the next, but no one can recall exactly how the melody went. My own wavering, insistent voice. What I sing makes the least sense of all. Everyone snaps at me that that isn't how it went. An overwhelming sense of alienation from my yesterday: surely my song is whatever I'm singing right now. The confused smile of my father, who is still holding his suitcase and feels out of place among all these women.

Comings, goings, comings, goings. I am constantly threatened that my parents will be told how badly I behave, and then they are told what a good girl I am. I believe both. And most of all summer, summer, the massive surge of a child's summer between four and five. Time without beginning or end. A boundless present: a raincoat I never take off. Where is it?

And mainly, above all: my Aunt Marie. We live to be together, day after day, always within eyeshot of each other. Grandma goes out to the fields, Aunt Marie looks after me. We never go anywhere. We never open the garden gate.

Of course, I understand this, because my aunt is a "voluntary prisoner" and I even know why. Because they stoned her in the village, on the green, with stones "big as a man's hand." It seems completely natural to me not to go into a village where you have been stoned; still, the idea of a stoning does not disturb me.

Our days are endless and our mutual bond is rich. We weed the vegetable garden, feed the hens, and draw with pastels. Aunt Marie teaches me German. On Saturdays my parents are always surprised how much I have learned and how many pictures I have drawn. I learn not words, but whole sentences, because Aunt Marie realized immediately that I have a God-given talent. Sentences like: "I'm fine, thank you," "I love you, Mommy and Daddy," or "Grandma and Aunt Marie are nice to me." I know lots of sentences already.

What we draw are more properly called "studies." Aunt Marie, you see, is a painter. She could not study painting; it is somehow connected with my mother. She threw her off her bike (my mother threw my aunt off, that is) and Aunt Marie got pneumonia. I do not understand this; it is a vortex of secretive pauses. I do not ask.

The studies are girls' profiles. I learn to draw heavy eyelids, drooping eyebrows, lips slightly parted. I learn the magic of complementary colors: blondes have blue eyes, brunettes have dark ones, and a redhead's are green, like a cat's. When the face is done, then comes the most important part: I am allowed to break off the tip of the pastel and crumble it. Then, with exceedingly gentle, intimate touches, we spread the dust out around the girl's head. The girls give off a fragile glow. We deposit them in a prewar candy box. What does "prewar" mean? I am learning to water the garden.

Am I happy? I don't know. I simply am. The eternal present's protective cocoon carries me through the days, whose succession I barely notice. The current of infinity surrounds me — the current of the commonplace.

I barely notice my grandmother, because it is harvest time and Grandma is constantly in the fields. She is a quiet, pious woman, who is a bit afraid (I don't know why) of my aunt. A fragment of one hot afternoon, what I can retain of my childhood memories at this remove.

Aunt Marie is having a "fit." She is running around the sitting room, shrieking. I do not understand her, because she is shrieking in German. I have not learned the sentences she shrieks. Grandma is crying quietly into her clasped hands. I crumble a salted crescent-roll into my milk. The crumbs float silently on the surface. Suddenly Grandma jumps out of her corner and, with a wildness I have never seen in her, shrieks and latches onto my aunt's hand.

"Marie! Don't raise your fist to the cross!" she implores. "Don't raise your fist against it!"

I watch her with interest as, with the full weight of her tiny, withered body, she hangs on to my aunt's arm, the one threatening the black crucifix. And then that scene too slides into oblivion.

But these animated outbursts are not very common. It is my conversations with Aunt Marie, as I remember it, that cover the greatest expanses of time. For we talk incessantly. The discussions are about our future, even though I don't have a future yet (what is a "future"?), so what we're talking about has to occur as soon as possible, preferably right away. Because Aunt Marie is strong, because an arc of solidarity shines bright between us, we have only to speak and it all becomes real.

"A painter?" Aunt Marie thoughtfully shakes her head. Absent-mindedly she shreds a pod into tiny bits. "A painter?"

We are talking about whether I will be a painter or a writer. We endlessly analyze which of the two possibilities is better. It is entirely possible that I will be both. No: my future is in me. I am already both.

"The main thing is to start soon," Aunt Marie insists. "There are whiz-kids everywhere these days. You mustn't delay!"

She pounds an earwig into the vegetable bed with a tool handle, and an s-shaped curl falls over her forehead. I have a curl like that too, but it's not as pretty yet. My mother is silly for cutting my hair like a boy's.

"You know about Cornelia, don't you? That famous five-year-old German singer? Who bought her mother a house with what they paid her for that song about the satin dress?"

I too have a pink satin dress; Aunt Marie made it for me. She wears long flounced skirts and every morning curls her short fountain of hair into "snail spirals." They bounce up and down across her forehead. She says that it's details like this that give us women our appeal. What is a "detail"? We often put snail spirals into our studies.

"You have to catch people's eyes!" Auntie insists angrily, thumping her hoe into the kohlrabi. "You've got to look pretty, even at your age! Does your mother think you're a little monkey? Is that what they call style in Prague? If you were mine, I'd have done things differently from the start!"

If you were mine: the other inexhaustible theme of our conversations. I'm already half hers anyway. A luminous twilight swallows the vegetable bed, the watered earth breathes around us, we pledge our troth to a secret life.

"I'd make you into a little princess!" says Auntie, plucking weeds. "I wouldn't leave you to rot in that darned Czechoslovakia of yours. We'd escape to Germany, find Franz, and he'd take care of us his way!"

When I live in Germany (with Auntie and Franz), I'm not called Dana like I am here. It's a silly name and it upsets my aunt. I have an old Germanic name: Saussika. I wear long flounced dresses. I have snail spirals, watercolors, a pallet and brushes — that's so I can learn to paint. I don't have to learn to write. Writing is from God. Neither Auntie nor I have any doubt that God is teaching me to write, today and every day.

"Once you're a little older," Auntie says, "you'll write something about me. You'll write my life as a novel. If I'm still breathing, if our good Lord hasn't released me from this scabby old world, then I'll illustrate it for you. And your novel will clear my name."

How old is Aunt Marie? To me she seems much younger than my mother (she is five years older); she's on a parallel track with me, a joyous geyser of the present gushing back into itself.

"You'll write my whole life in it. How Franz and me loved each other and how those pigs here stoned me. I'll give you a title for it. It'll be called *Meine Gespräche mit Tante Mitzi.* That means 'My Conversations with Aunt Mitzi.' It's a real good title for a book."

The sun sinks below the horizon and summer's freshness wafts in off the fields. We take the watering cans — I have the smaller one — and make beautiful dark stripes between the tomatoes.

"Just don't waste time! Every day matters. The earlier you make your mark, the better. We'll start right away. I'll tell you my whole story and you'll put the truth of it on paper, nice and pretty."

She gives me a penetrating look, silently counting something.

"How much longer till you learn to type? You're a clever girl. Maybe a year!"

At the moment I can hardly write three lines a day. No one could expect me to become a writer just like that. I can't be like Cornelia — a miracle at five. But people understand. After all, singing is different from writing.

"Another good title would be *Die Liebe ist ewig,* 'Love Is Eternal,' don't you think? Maybe not. They wouldn't believe you thought it up yourself. Too bad, because it's a pretty title. But everyone would say I gave it to you."

The subtitle will be "Through a Child's Eyes." What should I do? For now just listen and, most importantly, not close off my soul. God will take care of the rest.

"But will you promise not to betray me like everyone else? Do you swear cross your heart that you'll write about me?" Auntie asks doubtfully. "Will you promise? Nonsense! Promises, promises. Don't promise me anything."

Why not? I'll promise everything. The omnipresence of time, the everpresentness of my future guarantees that I will not be unfaithful. And do I truly believe in God? Of course. So I'll promise Him, not Auntie. Then it can never be taken back. I learn what an oath is.

"Raise your right hand! Two fingers together: like you and our good Lord. Repeat after me!"

We kneel in the beds of lettuce and bitter-smelling tomatoes. We rinse our hands, so as not to offer Our Lord our dirty fingers. Then both of us raise our hands at once to the heavens; Aunt Marie's voice shakes.

"Our Father, Who art in Heaven, I swear to You..."

I swear that I will be (that I am) a writer. I swear that I will write about my aunt, *Meine Gespräche mit Tante Mitzi — My Conversations with Aunt Marie.* No one, nothing will deter me from this, I swear.

Enter Grandma, coming down the watered path. She sees us, red with excitement, kneeling in the vegetable beds, but (as always) does not dare ask. We do not inform her of our oath. As if nothing has happened we pick up the watering cans and Auntie calls in a voice full of tears and triumph:

"Na komm, komm, Saussika, komm!"

I understand her, even though I have not yet learned this sentence. *Komm* means "come" and Saussika — that's me. I go into the house, cool in the evening shadows, and I burn with happiness and pride, as if it is not I who has just promised something to God, but God who has promised something to me. My entire future is in me. The tall, timeless pillar of omnipotence rises straight through me. I am my own time.

Then fragments I should remember, the seeds of my writerhood. Foremost is the story "About Franz," albeit sullied by thousands of asides, by the textual criticism of adulthood. I no longer live at the source, and alone I cannot see that original kernel of our *Talks.*

It is wartime and a German detachment has settled in her Sudeten village (what does "Sudeten" mean?). A young soldier,

Franz, falls in love with my Aunt Mitzi. My Aunt Mitzi falls in love with Franz. (An aside, defiling the original source: a proud old maid, she was thirty-two at the time.) It is a great love, infinite, eternal, and like everything that is truly great, it is beyond time's grasp. Franz is here for three weeks. When the detachment is ordered elsewhere, Franz swears an oath that after the war he will return for my aunt, and now I understand what an oath is. He gives her ten yards of yellow ribbon and ten yards of crimson. Yellow means jealousy and crimson — love. And then what?

Nothing. Still nothing. Nothing: room for a novel. Nine and a half years after the war, no news of Franz has ever come. Did he fall? No. Aunt Marie feels sure. If he had fallen, her heart would have told her, but her heart has said nothing of the sort. Franz therefore lives, in Germany, but because "shameful politics" rules the world, he cannot come for us and take us back with him forever.

Auntie knows that Franz still waits for her. Every once in a while he has German Radio play her a song. Anonymously, of course, because shameful politics would try to spoil even her last joy in life, if it (shameful politics) knew. The song is "Abend, oh Abend." That means: "Evening, Oh Evening." Franz would play it for my aunt on his harmonica as he stood beneath her window.

The second story, "About the Stoning," is much harder to make out. My aunt had cursed shameful politics out loud. It was in the village, in broad daylight. When they expelled the Germans (I see in my mind's eye how they were expelled, propelled through the village on a conveyor belt; I even see, hazily, a man giving them the final push), my aunt swore to take revenge on that man. I cannot know his name; I am still too young for that. I leave it for later; I do not insist on understanding my own novel all at once.

Auntie went to the village green, she stood there in broad daylight and said things for which "you get a rope around your neck" (do you have to wear it then?), but she, my Aunt Mitzi, was only stoned. Screaming, she fled, her hands covering her scalp, home to her house and there — here! she pounded her fist on the floor — she swore an oath never to set foot in the village again. A third oath! My novel will have sharp edges. It has been eight years since my aunt last set foot outside the gate.

And now my own story, a link of authenticity. Vaccination, the summer I am there: "A Story about Vaccination." A loudspeaker circles the house like a gadfly: "All citizens are required to report for vaccinations!" My aunt and I stand hidden behind the hedge, and she urges me on:

"Saussika! Throw that rotten potato at them! You're just a kid, nothing will happen to you!"

Whenever the car goes by, she picks me up enough for me to see over the hedge and I heave a potato after the car. I only hit them twice. Auntie kisses me affectionately and enthusiastically; squatting beneath a sky of Jericho roses, we hug each other and laugh out loud, insanely, in a fabulous intimacy.

Then, the next day, a man with a scar is standing at the gate. He is shouting and Auntie is shouting too. An ambulance is parked in front of the house all morning. The man chases my aunt around the kitchen; she hangs on to the curtains, white-fingered. Will they take her away? Will they stone her? Grandma, weeping, boils water. The man ties my aunt to a chair with his belt. A woman pricks a needle into Auntie's skinny forearm, into its gelatinous, aging flesh. Then my aunt lies down until evening, just staring at the low ceiling. "Saussika, never forgive anyone for anything!"

And meanwhile, during, before, afterward, a hot July. The glowing, rolling wave of a child's summer, a fount of eternity, time from nowhere to nowhere. Franz loves my aunt, Grandma was born old, I am a writer.

The last story entrusted to my pen: a man "courted" my aunt. A scene of them walking together across cornfields. He picks her some wild red poppies. "My beautiful Marie, I should have looked more closely. What's done is done, I pointed at the wrong one." I realize — but only very hazily — that this man is probably my father, but my aunt will not be more specific and I do not ask. In the end, all writerhood is half-light and speculation. And again the summer, summer, summer surging past, back and forth.

Then one day I run in from the garden with an egg in my hands. I have found it lying by the fence. I am in the hallway when a loud whisper from inside takes me by surprise. I peer into the kitchen: my mother is sitting there, angrily whispering to my grandma. My aunt is sleeping next door in the sitting room, as she does every day. It is midday, filtered gray through the brown curtains; no one has seen me yet.

"No!" my mother shouts in a whisper. "I've heard quite enough already! And I want my child left out of it!"

She sits bent almost double, her fingers darting out from her palms, one after the other. (An aside: my mother's age-old habit of supporting her words by toting up individual points, even when there are no points and nothing anywhere in her speech that can be counted.)

"A complete crackpot!" She shakes her thumb at Grandma. "Raving mad. For Christ's sake, the kid isn't even five yet!"

My mother is different from us. She's Praguified. She has an actress's clear diction, which carries, even in a whisper, across the hall.

"But ... but you know how she is, hon..." Grandma sighs.

"So she's bats, fine, but I won't have her playing around with my daughter's mind! Come on, do you know who they pray for together? For the Germans we expelled in '46! For collaborators! She may be the official village idiot, but this could cause a real mess in Prague! And who'll pay for it? Her? Not likely. It'll be me, as always!"

Grandma tilts her head. "You know how it is ... you know..."

"How old is she?" Mother's index finger shoots out. "Has her watch stopped or something?"

A golden fly has settled on my shoe. My impulsive mother is shaking all her fingers at once.

"What's she waiting for? What? For that ladykiller to come back for her? That slick Kraut? She's past forty! Time to have a look at the calendar!"

Grandma is wringing her fingers.

"Still ... how can you take it away from her? How can you?"

"So we're just supposed to keep acting in her little play, pretending time doesn't exist? That it's stopped, for her sake? Time marches on! Time flies! No carriage waits forever! My child can't stay here, not another day!"

I stand and I hear. I feel nothing and I think of nothing else. Perhaps God is writing inside me in his special script, who knows; I see, I hear, the sitting room door opens.

"No! I won't let you take her away from me! Not her!"

Like oil on water Aunt Mitzi, in her nightgown, steps out of the half-light.

"I won't let you! I won't! Don't take her away from me!"

Her hair is unkempt and she is shouting like when they came to give her the injection.

"You want to take away everything I have, everything! Why can you always do everything, and I can't do anything? Except follow you around and pick up what you drop. How come you get to be a little lady from the city while I just rot here like a dead dog?"

My mother the Praguer, my coiffed city dweller, snaps back immediately.

"Then you should have had your own child, instead of messing up mine! Whose fault is it anyway that you've got soup for brains!"

"Girls! Girls! For the love of God!" Grandma sobs. Then my aunt notices me standing in the dim hallway, and in a single jump she has me in her arms.

"I love her!" she shrieks in a thin voice. "I love her more than all of them do! I got nothing else left, nothing in the whole world!"

"Look, an egg!" I'm shrieking too, and I hold it up in one hand, so my aunt won't crush it. "An egg!"

And again: oblivion, the luscious rippling of time's languid body, that day or any other, an egg — that one, or any other — is hard-boiled, and my aunt makes lines with it, shifts it behind her back, the egg disappears ... aha! Where is it now? ... like the moon I circle my aunt, laughing, my aunt runs round the sitting room and Grandma, happy to have peace in the house again, watches. The radio plays "Abend, oh Abend." My aunt gazes knowingly at me over my mother's bristly scalp. God is teaching me to write.

But in the end, my mother doesn't take me away — no, she takes herself and Grandma away to the fair at Jevíčko. It's a tremendously lengthy trip: they won't be back till tomorrow morning, but they have piled up provisions for us as if we were arctic explorers in winter. My mother starts the car with her whole body — she does everything with her whole body — she grips the wheel like reins, the car breaks into a gallop, and my grandma draws a large cross with her finger on the rear windshield.

No sooner has the car vanished around the curve than I begin to change completely and unhesitatingly into Saussika. Auntie and I throw open the wardrobes and play "dress up." I choose a pink satin dress, sewn at the miraculous Cornelia's behest, and my aunt tries to curl my hair, which has grown out nicely over the summer. The s-curl, which we have hidden from my mother and which my aunt combs out for me with a barrette, hangs down to my nose and tickles my forehead. Finally I am myself, we no longer have to hide the fact that I am a young German beauty and not an ugly little boy from Prague.

"And that man, you know, the one I told you about ... in the cornfield ..."

Today my aunt is unusually confiding. She combs my hair and fills in details for my novel; they'll certainly come in handy some day. I know who she means. The man who pointed at the wrong one.

"Know what I said to him? Guess! What would you say?"

I don't know. "I don't know," I say. Now my aunt is brushing her own hair. I sniff it with delight: a scent of femininity and beauty wafts from it like from a prewar candy box.

"Then listen up, I'll give you another bit for your pen. I took the bouquet of poppies from him, because a girl can always take a bouquet. But nothing more! Remember that! If they send you a jewel, then you have to write a card immediately, saying you're honored but it's too great a present, and you're returning it with thanks."

Auntie has a lilac blouse with balloon sleeves. She has a skirt with flounces all the way to the floor. We're each more beautiful than the other. We're the most beautiful people on earth. Now we've become the studies.

"My boy, I tell him, don't be disappointed with my answer, because I'm telling you it just can't be. Do you know what Franz gave me as a good-bye present? Ten yards of yellow ribbon. And do you know what yellow stands for, my boy?"

"Jealousy," I answer for my father in the corn. What does "jealousy" mean? My aunt nods.

"And crimson stands for love. You think that love can disappear, admit it, don't you? Then you're a poor thing indeed, my boy; I can't even tell you how sorry I feel for you in my heart. Rubbish! True love is infinite. Love is eternal, my boy!"

Yes. How else could it be? How else, other than eternal? I find this notion more obvious than it would seem — thanks less to the concept of love than to the concept of eternity. I don't trip on time's protrusions. It carries me like an escalator: Whatever is, is. If something disappears, it's gone from my sight and thoughts at once. I move onward, standing firm: I do not leave my step.

In the afternoon I sleep, we play Old Maid a thousand times in a row, we water the flowers, and finally it's time for hide-

and-seek. How do you play hide-and-seek with a child? I sneak behind a bush, my aunt pretends to look for me for a while, and when she finds me, we both happily let out a squeal. The sun rolls lazily down toward the fields. There will be cake for dinner.

"No standing near home base, or I won't play! Yoo-hoo! Hide, quickly, Saussika!"

Suddenly it hits me that there's a small hollow in the woodshed behind the logs. I know it because I look for eggs in there. It's where a fat white hen does her laying. The thrill enlivens me, and while my aunt counts aloud I run into the woodshed and work my way underneath the wood.

"Nine and ten and ready or not, here I come!"

My hideout offers an exceptionally miserable view. All I can see is the flounces, the hem of my aunt's skirt swishing and fluttering down the path.

"Yoo-hoo! Where are you?" my aunt calls. The hem flaps over by the bushes. She must be checking all the hiding places we've used, but because the garden is practically all within arm's reach, there are only a handful of them. I quiver with laughter. The hem runs off again.

"Saussika! Saussika!"

I don't answer. A small chicken walks solemnly past me. At eye height I see her taloned feet. My aunt is so close I could almost touch her.

"Come on! Where are you? Hey, answer me!"

Perish the thought. This is the first time I've won a game. I'm bewitched, an egg hard-boiled.

"I'm done playing! You hear me? Come out right now!"

A car roars through the village. Two lights fly through the earthy twilight, lick my burrow, and fly away again.

"Dana! Dana! Where are you?"

This evening, dim and distant, is the horizon of my remembering. Only since then has my time taken on the illusion of direction. Everything lying below it is a featureless confusion.

"Help! Hey! Help! Someone, help me!"

I am lying on my stomach. A stick of wood presses into my rear. My aunt's somewhat indistinct voice now sounds far away. Another car roars by. I have no intention of coming out until I'm properly found. I have always been found, up till now.

"Help! Help!"

I hear the gate creak. I haven't seen the flounces in a long time. Everything is silent.

It's dusk already. Sparks of cold rise from the nearby stream. The lengthening shadows of the beanpoles crawl into the woodhouse, and then suddenly everything goes out — curls up and goes out .... I sleep.

When I wake up, a bright light is shining, piercing through my tightly closed eyelids down to my throat. Something rudely invades my hiding place: a man's scarred hands. A big man in overalls grabs me and pulls me out by the neck like a lizard.

"Here you go, here's your 'kidnapped girl'! 'Kidnapped'! Ha!"

The man grabs me by the shoulders without any of the tenderness I'm used to, picks me up, and roughly shakes me in the air.

"This time keep an eye on her, you silly goat! Because of you I had to stop the winnower! Know what that'll cost me? Do you?"

I start to sniffle a bit from the shock. In the light of the huge flashlight I finally find my aunt, but she's not looking at me. Both her palms are covering her face and her shoulders are shaking. A wilted s-curl hangs across her skinny fingers. Suddenly, with a mighty swing, the man swats me across the behind.

"You both deserve a swift kick in the ass!" he sniggers. "I'd whip this little brat till she couldn't sit for a week. But your daddy's too classy for that, right?"

He sniggers again, lights a cigarette, and looks us over in disbelief.

"Jesus, where did you think you were going in those clothes? To a ball? You look like a couple old ladies!"

The dark and cold make me tremble. I'm bawling loudly. The man picks up his flashlight, spits into the aster bed, and swaggers off toward the gate. He jumps on his tractor, the engine barks, and the man leans out of its clamor for one last word:

"And if you don't come for your next vaccination, then I'll vaccinate you myself with a dung pitchfork! Don't forget!"

Then he leaves us in the darkness. I sob and stumble as my aunt drags me into the house.

What next? What now? What's about to happen to me? My aunt silently removes my satin dress, silently combs the wood shavings from my hair. I sit in the empty wash-tub and wait for my aunt to pour the water. Why is it different today? Other times my aunt pours the water down the side of the tub and only then, with a huge laugh, throws my naked, wriggling body in. Something is happening, I know it — like a cat I can feel the earthquake coming, I am walking across a bridge with no foundations, and then suddenly, impulsively, from the empty washtub I say:

"There was a goat in our garden today!"

It isn't true. What would a goat have been doing in the garden? It is a baldfaced lie.

Without looking at me or saying a word, my aunt scrubs my back as if she were washing the floor. To my amazement, I hear myself spouting meaningless sentences about the goat. I mix together memories from another time, a fairytale, and labored lying; my imagination struggles mightily, I swim against the current without knowing why. Why am I spinning this tall tale, which has no rhyme or reason? My aunt isn't even listening; she is scrubbing, lips pursed, letting me pile lie upon lie.

"It was bleating like this: meh, meh!" I run, wet and naked, around the sitting-room, poking my imaginary horns into the darkness and bleating at the top of my lungs, "Meh!"

Is this the gift of words? Why do I suddenly sound different? I stuff my imagination's phantom with words, wrapping the goat in the fur of speech; with growing anxiety and unexpected drudgery I spin my first independent text. Is writerhood really so arduous? So oppressive, so precarious? Distressed, I drown out the silence, which confuses me; in his trained hand, God writes me a message from the future, the promise's knot tightens ever so slightly, but still my aunt does not answer.

Finally, numb and worn out with fibbing, I fall into the featherbed, burrowing into it like a den. Now comes "Abend, oh Abend," like every day. When we say our prayers together I will be cleansed of the imaginary goat and will fall asleep ever so quickly. But Aunt Marie does not sit down by my side. She stands erect over the bed, a lit candle in her hands, like a prophet, and for the first time that evening she speaks to me.

"I don't love you anymore," she says slowly, raising the candle a bit. "I can't love you ever again. I won't tell anyone what you did to me. I'll be like always. I'll cook for you, sew for you ... but I can never, ever love you like I did before."

Then she turns and disappears back into the darkness. The small candle stands next to the chamber-pot, so I won't be afraid to use it in the night. In the night: how to describe the chilling draft of the night across my entire body? Grandma's bed is empty; Grandma is at the fair in Jevíčko. Everpresent eternity has ended forever.

In the morning my mother and grandmother return from Jevíčko, tanned and happy. The car is loaded to the roof with watermelons. They feel a bit guilty for having left us "alone" for so long, but, warmed by the zephyrs of other worlds, they are packed with news and very cheerful. My mother flashes with all her fingers, crams the car full of vegetables, throws my things into it any which way, and cuts an unbelievably large bouquet of dahlias. Her short hair whips around her head with each exclamation.

Then there is much kissing: Grandma kisses me, Aunt Marie kisses me, I kiss both of them, they kiss my mother, thank you so much! for taking such good care of me! I haven't been a nuisance? of course not! and we jump into the car, but I forgot my doggy, so quickly back, until my mother steps wholeheartedly on the gas and the car ecstatically carries us away.

Can we truly bear the memory of love's finiteness and still preserve our identity, that vertical current of eternity, a pemmican that resists cold and time, the heart of a divine game? The car carries me off through the hot, dusty September; like a rally driver, my mother barrels between the sleeping granaries and I am no longer myself. I am not suffering from the woes of love — the depths of my young ego are still too centripetal for love to be possible. I am suffering from surprise. The happy time of temporal weightlessness, swimming while standing on my head, is irretrievably gone. Flung from my orbit, I fly off sharply on my own. As I take on direction, the overload grows. My past detaches from me with a rumble and shoots off into the clouds; the stages fall away and instantly burn up, my body bursts through into the formless future, into today, furrows behind me, swirling fog before me; the lights in the distance are fiery streaks behind my back, nothing lasts even a moment, and yet my speed is still increasing.

"Aunt Marie doesn't love me anymore," I say suddenly, just as the car flies into a curve. A truck whizzes past us like a hornet. My mother turns the wheel sharply, leans out the window, and shouts, pointlessly, at the clattering back of the truck, which is already disappearing down the road:

"You idiot!" she calls out. "I hope you kill yourself!"

Then she starts the car again and, before her wrath fades, she exclaims:

"I'm never taking you there again! She's really messed you up!"

She never did take me there again. I never saw Aunt Marie after that. She is still alive. I am thirty, she is almost seventy, and Cornelia, if she is still among us, is swimming toward the eddies of old age. Twenty-six years have elapsed since I passed the starting line that night.

What happened to the contract concluded in the tomato patch? God fulfilled his promise: I am a writer — but not even I can untie the knot of an oath. Twenty-six years later, I am discharging my debt and finishing these *Gespräche mit Tante Mitzi, My Conversations with Aunt Marie*. But I won't let her know. It wouldn't mean anything to her anymore. That narrow band of clear summer, when we lived together in a common time, has ended forever. Now we each have our own direction and speed, and when there is no common moment, there is no room for meaning. Only one thing remains, and it is always the same: the anxious call of love, which for a moment is eternal, an illegible letter tossed against the current that silently carries us away.

A Letter for President Eisenhower

Sometimes it seems that everything's pretend. That it's only a gesture that misses the mark. I am ten years old.

It is the year synthetic materials hit Prague. A new store, Plastik, appeared on Wenceslas Square and there are lines in front of it every day. Everything still amazes us: parkas, nylon bags, statues made from PVC.

One day my mother returns victoriously with plastic cutlery that looks like wood. The marvel is that the wood isn't wood, just like the statues' marble isn't marble. It is a collective plastic attack that will soon pass — within a year, the cutlery will end up in the trash — but now we raise the strangely weightless knife up to the light, the knife tips upward like a finger pointing somewhere else and, marveling, we fall under the spell of its artifice.

One morning Comrade Principal comes for me and for my best friend Hana. To the envy of all our classmates, she plucks us out of a test and leads us to her office in silence. Hana's dark ponytail trembles. Hana is perpetually alarmed, always more exemplary than me.

"Our school," the principal says sternly, "has decided to write to President Eisenhower."

Small, bent, and wrinkled, she is sitting in her army jacket behind a large desk. To my horror I see that she is holding our notebooks. Hana's are much more attractive than mine. Hana has terrific handwriting. She gets to write for the school bulletin board. Her handwriting is just like her: tiny, well formed. Always the same, tidy.

"The West," the principal continues, "is secretly preparing for war. They want to stab us in the back. But we won't let anyone take peace away from us!"

She picks up a composition I recognize, and the shock makes my heart leap in my chest. It is my contribution to the Young Writers competition, which won second prize in the Prague 10 district. It is called "A Merry Christmas Party."

"You," the principal points her finger, "you will write the letter. And you: copy it over in your best handwriting. I want to see it before vacation. You have two weeks."

She opens a drawer and spends a long time looking for something. She seems to have forgotten about us. I don't dare utter a word. Suddenly she stands up and stares me straight in the eye.

"It's high time the truth be told!" she shouts as if from a deep sleep. The tips of my fingers tingle with excitement. The principal hands me an outline.

*

I fly home, riding the crest of the moment. Outline, point one: greeting. Dear President Eisenhower! Outline, point four. The horrors of war. Like in Soviet films. Signature: We, the children of Czechoslovakia. And it is I who was given this historic task!

Fourth grade took something out of me. Just last year I swam through life like a fish through water. Now I'm a dry cork on the surface. I tread water and try to get down into it. Life's everyday certainties are irrevocably gone.

Everything is just pretend. Since I can still faithfully imitate the loud, pudgy little girl I was not so long ago, no one has caught on yet. For example, everyone believes I love writing essays, but actually it bores me to death. My "Merry Christmas Party" was made up out of thin air. About thin-air kids doing thin-air things. In spite of this, everyone believes I'm going to be a writer. I'm sentenced to fiction for life.

It doesn't bother me. I play laboriously at playing. Sometimes I sense adults' fleeting anxiety that everything's already happened. I secretly hope for a "jolt," for a catapult of transformation, as if I were a larva that ravenous inertia drives forth from its cocoon.

Is this my jolt? Presenting mankind's credentials in a letter? It's high time the truth be told! For ten days I write as if in a fever.

First I describe rivers of blood. I awaken the conscience of the American government. I speak with Eisenhower as an equal, but then behind all mankind's back I chew on my pen. I cross out whole mountains of pages, I don't sleep, I fall exhausted at the foot of the White House steps. Hana's mother says the whole thing is pretty stupid. Hana, of course, repeats this to me.

Finally the letter is ready. It contains the horrors of war, as depicted in films. It contains many, many exclamation points. It contains the sentence: "After all, I myself am still a child!" Hana contends that it is too long, but doesn't put up a fight. She copies it perfectly, without a single mistake.

That evening I find an excuse to go out, and I run over to Hana's. My authorial pride goads me on. I long to see that beautifully copied letter again. I want to touch it before Eisenhower does. To weigh in my hands the paper confection in which my challenge to the White House will arrive.

Hana awkwardly lets me in. Usually we run right to her room, but today we stand in the hallway, shifting from foot to foot, as if on a train. Suddenly, through the wall, I hear an explosion of laughter and the voice of Hana's mother. She's reading my letter to her guests. "We children are too weak; our hands cannot carry bombs," she declaims in a flat, cadaverous voice. That's how the TV comedian they call the Sad Man speaks. Hana doesn't laugh, but her tidy, perfidious face makes it clear that she completely agrees with the antics on the other side of the wall.

"My parents insist that the principal's crazy," she says defensively, looking straight at me with prim courage.

"You're the one who's crazy! Just wait till there's a war!"

I turn on my heel and trot down the dark hallway. Hana quietly closes the door as waves of laughter billow forth. Blinded by my humiliation, I vanish into the darkness.

For the three days left till the end of the year, we don't speak to each other. On Friday, on the very brink of vacation, she stops me to say she's not my friend anymore. Stunned, caught unawares, I say I don't really care. It's all over between us, she says. I say that's fine. Hana heads home with an even stride, trailing straight A's from her beribboned folders.

I flee into the coatroom and cry a little. It's my pride that hurts, not my heart. This year I have no heart. The principal meets me in front of the school and stops me with a stern gesture. She stares at me for a while, as if trying to remember who I could possibly be. Then she shakes her head with a strange horselike motion, strides off and, as she walks away, says forcefully: "The letter's fine."

July is desolate. I wander listlessly around the garden with nothing to do. A dull film lies spread over everything; under its protective coating the summer fades like a chest beneath a plastic slipcover in a deserted room. I try to think about President Eisenhower, but since the incident with Hana a film has spread over him too. The chill gray days slide by.

On Sunday evening someone rings the bell. The caretaker, Miss Zámský, runs to the gate. Boredom keeps me eternally draped out the window, and so I see a burly old man come in. He has a cane and keeps coughing. Behind him walks a sturdy, dark-skinned girl. She furrows the ground with her dark, indifferent eyes, and scowls.

"Hello!" Miss Zámský shouts, and she waves at me. "We've brought you a friend! She's from Votice! Show yourself to the young lady, Sasha!"

*

The next day they put us together. It is wet, and we're wearing sweats and jackets. We wander here and there near the house. Sasha is glum.

"How old are you?" I ask.

"Just turned thirteen."

Even under the jacket I can see that she has breasts. She doesn't look at me. She doesn't look at anything. She just goes where the path takes her, with a heavy, uninterested tread.

"Are you starting eighth grade?"

"No."

"Why not? If you're thirteen ...."

We walk past the bench. Mr. Zámský lets out a guffaw. He slaps Sasha on the rear and for about the fifth time says:

"Thatta girl! And what a piece of girl she is, huh?"

Mr. Zámský gives me the jitters. His big head is continually shaking. His tongue hangs out of his mouth and his eyes look like they're swimming in formaldehyde.

"Is that your uncle? Is he nice to you?"

Sasha just shrugs her shoulders. "He's nuts."

My feet are killing me. I'd like to go home. I have no idea what to say, but the footpath pulls me onward like a tugboat.

"What do you like to play?"

"You won't tell my aunt?"

I raise two fingers, wet with my saliva. "Promise."

"Lovers," Sasha says. I am dumbfounded.

"But ... how?" I ask. It begins to rain again. Sasha looks around.

"Come over behind these trees," she whispers. We step into cool, damp shadows. Rainwater drips down our necks. Sasha doesn't hesitate. She bends over and kisses me on the lips. Her mouth is slippery with baby oil.

"That's how," she says flatly. I guess that's all there is to it. We run out into the rain and then play rummy with Miss Zámský until evening.

After that we're together all the time. We never leave the garden; we play constantly. At what? At being lovers. Sasha doesn't want to play anything else. How? It's simple. We walk through the birch trees, hand in hand, and give each other kisses. Do I like it? Not at all. At ten I have finally left cuddliness behind and they won't get me back so quickly. Besides, there's something missing for me in this game, but I don't know what it is.

"And what are we called?"

"What is who called?"

"Ow, why'd you bite me?! I mean the lovers!"

Without names it just won't work. A name is always more than a body. Sasha licks a blade of grass and concentrates on tickling the inside of my ear. I squirm, dissatisfied.

"So are we going out with each other? And will we get married someday? And have children? Huh?"

Who knows. Sasha never asks things like this. The world around Sasha stands still. I have a Young Writers silver medal and I know full well that the world is a story, a finger pointing somewhere else: a direction.

"So let's make something up!"

"Why? I don't want to."

"If I make something up, will you play it with me?"

Sasha doesn't know. It's all the same to her. She stops tickling me and starts single-mindedly squashing ants with her fingernail.

The next day I'm in the garden at eight. Furiously I stomp outside the Zámskýs' ground-floor window. Sasha is sleeping and doesn't want to get up, but I'm stomping like a real live elephant.

I have a story! Last night I couldn't fall asleep until two. A multitude of versions ran through my head. I'm as prolific as Adam in Paradise. I am amazed how easy it is to create new worlds. By the time sleep finally overtook me I had decided with solemn finality who Sasha and I really were.

From the window, Mr. Zámský threatens me with his cane; my noise annoys him. Sasha yawns. She takes ages eating breakfast. Finally we're out behind the birch trees. Mumbling, I explain her role. I know everything, absolutely everything! I (he) am called Mount Everest. Sasha (she) is Kilimanjaro.

There are two famous mountain climbers. They bear the names of the mountains they have climbed. Never in their lives have they met, but the world considers them merciless rivals. There is but one unconquered mountain left in all the world. It is the highest of them all and it has sent hundreds of climbers to their deaths. In the language of its country — Himalayan, I suspect — it is called the Mountain of Mountains.

Both decide to climb it. The whole world waits with baited breath to see who will be the first to raise the flag. The reporters are frantic, every transmitter is straining its ears. But shortly before they set out, a shock hits.

At the foot of the Mountain, Everest discovers the astounding truth. The whole world thinks this is a battle of man against man. Except Kilimanjaro is not a man.

Sasha: I only played this silly game for your sake. If you'd known I was a girl, you would never have competed against me.

Mount Everest (horrified): Kilimanjaro, I warn you — the Mountain of Mountains is the end of the earth! At the summit there is nothing but sheer frost.

The ascent begins. Step by step the way grows harder. The sky is like a white abyss and the world is so tense it forgets to breathe. The most frightening part of the Mountain draws near, the Wall of Death. No one, except Sasha and me, suspects the truth.

From that day on, the game takes an unexpected turn. At the end of the garden is a steep hill. The ground here is perpetually moist, covered with brushwood. It becomes the Wall of Death. We press through the bushes on our bellies; a mountain hurricane rips us asunder, thorns catch on our sweatpants. The Young Writer has turned a fin-de-siècle stroll in the park into a military exercise.

Most of all, our love is now different. There's no more kissing, thank God. Love is no longer a perpetual dance in a circle. It's a contest, it's agony. It's a finger pointing straight up — a direction! We crawl across the icy plain, exhausted. Embraces are out of the question, and anyway we are kept apart by layers of walrus skin. At these heights, a kiss without an oxygen mask spells death.

*

My parents are just thankful I'm playing and not lazing around the apartment looking bored. Two or three times they invite Sasha over for a snack, but in the house she turns glum again.

One evening my mother says Sasha is a dim bulb.

"She's got breasts big enough to be nursing, but every year she's got September makeup exams around her neck."

It doesn't make any sense to me. Sasha doesn't seem at all dim. On the contrary, she's fabulous. For example, she figured out how to freeze all by herself. I have never seen anyone freeze, so I have nothing to compare it to — but she can stiffen up like an icicle. She says I have to massage her with snow. Everest diligently rubs her hands, calloused by her coat fasteners, but Kilimanjaro does not wake up.

"Kiss me!" she hisses suddenly, still unconscious, her eyelids squeezed shut.

How do I know that the fateful moment has come? Like the snake-prince, I can see in the dark. I know things I've never encountered. With a single tug I rip off my oxygen mask. Everest falls head over heels in love.

The elderberry thicket closes over us. The stillness rumbles like a cracked bell, and the distant roar of avalanches gradually falls silent. Face to face with the sheer frost of death, Everest comes to know the terror of love. Practically without touching her, in a panic, he kisses her frozen face. Sasha immediately opens her eyes, and — although she knows I don't like it — the cunning girl licks me all over.

One evening there's a commotion downstairs. Sasha and I secretly peer through the window. Miss Zámský is chasing her brother around the kitchen; when he stops and cowers in horror against the wall, she swipes at him with a broom and, his hand shaking, he parries with his cane.

"You pig, shame on you!" she screams, swinging the broom round her head. "I'll throw you out of the house! Go back to Votice, you pig! Bet *they* don't want you either, you swine!"

She throws a brush at him. Mr. Zámský bursts through the door and makes his getaway. Sasha's eyes are shining. "I know why my aunt's upset!" she whispers. She bites her fingers so hard she leaves red welts on them, and brushes against me, giggling with excitement.

By the end of the week Sasha starts to rebel. We're all scratched up, we've broken our nails, and under our sweats our knees are thoroughly bruised. We've already climbed a slippery path along the Wall of Death, where the brushwood straggles to the ground. Sasha grumbles that she's lost interest.

I understand. After all, we're always playing the same thing. What's more attractive in love than the starting line? Again and again I wind the hands back to zero. Sasha freezes, Everest stands over her. The circulation of his blood pauses, like a paternoster grinding to a halt. This helping of emotion is quite enough for me, but Sasha is still grousing. She wants to know when we're going to get to the top.

The worst thing is that I don't know myself. The Young Writer is stuck in a creative crisis. I dragged us out to the ends of the earth and for a week I've held us there like a customs official. Just short of the goal my imagination has run dry. What awaits love at the summit of the Mountain of Mountains?

I compress my feelings like gas in a cylinder. I cross out the kisses; we're fighting for every gasp of air. The Mountain belches frost. I camp just shy of the summit, lacking the courage for that final step.

"I'm not playing!" Sasha pouts. Spitefully she sticks a thorn through my sweats. I beg her — just one more time. We both roll down to the fence; relieved, I slip back under the starting line of love and once again I'm crawling along on my belly like a newt.

On Sunday Sasha gets the flu. I can't see her and I'm desperate. I thrash around the apartment like a Christmas carp in a trough, I talk back, cut people off, and am so nasty that my mother ironically asks me:

"Do you love her so much you can't spend even one day apart?"

The question takes me by surprise. I don't love Sasha at all! It would never occur to me to love Sasha! Everest loves Kilimanjaro with the insanity of pure frost, but it has nothing to do with Sasha and me. We are mere players — a finger pointing somewhere else. We are only representatives, even if I don't know what of.

A numb tension dogs me all day. I read a little, but made-up stories irritate me. I stuff myself with cookies. Finally, just before supper, I get an idea for the next act of our play.

The exhausted Kilimanjaro is asleep in the cliff grotto. Everest sets out for the summit. He stands right below it. One more step and he could leave his thumbprint upon the very apex of the world. The lofty vacuum turns his blood to foam. Everest is alone like no one anywhere ever. He sits down on a ledge and takes out a piece of stationery. Beloved Kilimanjaro!

The love letter is an utterly alien genre for me. Laboriously I hunt for sentences to borrow, cobbling them together into something exceedingly odd. I don't believe what comes out of my pen. What I understand perfectly as a mute feeling is, when put into words, even thinner air than my Christmas Party.

Kilimanjaro! It is high time the truth be told. Until today I did not know what love was! ... They call me to supper, three times. Woodenly I stack line upon line. I love you. Meanwhile, the spinach on my plate is getting cold. Till I die I will love only you. The fourth time around, they hound me to supper.

Next, I figure out how we can correspond properly this far above sea level. With the help of some string, of course! I run downstairs. Miss Zámský is in the kitchen, curlers in her hair.

I'm hopping with impatience, I've explained it to her so many times! I'm even shouting. Miss Zámský wants to know why I don't just hand her the letter. With a speed borne of exasperation I rattle it off again. Miss Zámský asks: And what kind of game is it? Finally she throws up her hands and goes to wake Sasha up.

I stand on the balcony, tying the string. Carefully I lower the letter. WRITE BACK IMMEDIATELY! Everest adds. I mope around upstairs, trying to hypnotize the twilight. Hurrah! Sasha's hand sticks out from the rocky grotto. She attaches a note:

"My temperture's allmost normal. My aunts going to the movies tomorow so if you want come over."

As if to spite me, the heat today is like a frying pan. The sun beats against the closed windows. The basement apartment is oppressive and stifling. Mr. Zámský is asleep in a chair in the garden, and Sasha is sitting on her bed in a rumpled nightgown.

"Do you still feel sick?"

"Uh-uh."

"Still have a temperature?"

"M-hm."

Suddenly I don't know what to say. I stand up and look around. Most of all I'd like to crawl right into playing, like a hand into a glove.

"So are we going to play? Like always?"

"Hey, could you bring me something to drink?"

"I'll bring it to you when we pretend."

"What do you mean, pretend? I'm dying of thirst!"

"So pretend like he's coming back to free her from the snow."

Everest brings her warm lemonade in a plastic glass; even Miss Zámský has had a plastic attack, only she doesn't have a refrigerator. He finds Kilimanjaro sleeping. No, she's frozen. Everest stands for a while, completely beside himself. Then he puts the glass aside and begins to massage the forearms of this victim of the Mountain.

"Kilimanjaro! Don't die!" he whispers — today he's not at all convincing.

The victim opens one eye slightly: "Got the drink?"

She gulps it down at once and wipes the spills off her nightgown.

"You know what you have to do!" she says, and freezes. Mount Everest takes his time. It's not easy to introduce sheer frost into hundred-degree heat. Sasha breathes loudly. The hairs on her neck glisten gold with sweat. Everest still cannot get into the role. Finally he leans over, perplexed. A dying arm grabs him around the throat. He didn't expect this; his legs slide out from under him and he topples headlong into the featherbed.

When a shadow crosses the window, Everest's first fear is that they will find him in the Zámskýs' bed in his sneakers. He jumps up and comes to attention like an army officer. Mr. Zámský is squatting outside, tapping on the glass and snickering.

"Go jump in a lake, old man!" Sasha says irritably.

"What's he want with us?"

Sasha puts on an idiotic expression:

"Go on, girls, that's right, do it!"

Then she tumbles back into the featherbed and snores. Mr. Zámský shuffles inside. He slaps me on my rear and sits down on the bed.

"Well, girls! Want to look at some pictures? Not a word to Miss Z.! She doesn't need to know everything, right, girls?"

Sasha is snoring like a steam engine. At the same time she is nudging me in the back with her foot. The fever has unleashed her somehow. Mr. Zámský pulls out a tattered book.

"Come on, girls, let's have some fun together! After all, I saw you — you know how to have fun!"

Sasha leans forward on the mattress and props her chin on his shoulder. Cardboard figures stand out from the page: a ballerina and a man holding a hat right below his belly. Strings hang down beneath them. Mr. Zámský winks at us. He pulls one string and the ballerina raises her leg up high. It turns out she isn't wearing any panties.

"Hey!" Sasha yelps, and she rips the book away from her uncle. She pulls another string. The man jerks his arms away.

"Give it back! Sasha!" Mr. Zámský shouts. Sasha jumps around the bed, the bed flexes like a trampoline. Panicking, her uncle grabs hold of the footboard.

"Get over here!" Sasha calls to me. I hesitate, but she holds out her hand. I don't recognize her at all today. Hastily I kick off my shoes and clamber over.

"Sasha! You little devil!" Mr. Zámský moans. He's afraid to stand up and can barely hold on to the rail. I'm jumping as well. It's easier than keeping my balance. Suddenly a strange hotness enters me. Sasha jerks on the string, the man thrusts his naked belly onto the ballerina, and we both yelp, "Whee!"

"You! Little girl! Make her give back the book!"

I'm choking in the stifling room. I don't recognize either Sasha or myself. I jump and shriek with all my might, "Whee!"

Suddenly Sasha yells, "Auntie's coming!" and quick as a flash tosses the book behind the bed. Mr. Zámský is horribly frightened. He leaps up, dropping his cane, but leaves it lying on the floor and flees. I too am horribly frightened; I've turned white as a sheet. Sasha laughs wildly and burrows her nose into the featherbed.

"There's no one coming, don't worry. I just said that so he'd leave. Come crawl under the featherbed so he can't see us!"

She picks up the book and blows off the dust. She nods to me and pats the place next to her.

"I'm still going to tell my aunt on him tonight!"

She sits up, takes off her nightgown, and spreads her legs apart. Carefully she examines the picture and then between her own thighs. Everest stands on the bed; he can't move, must be frozen.

"Come on already!" Sasha snaps at me. The featherbed rolls over us like an avalanche.

As I run up the steps, lightning flashes. It gives the impression that evening has arrived early today.

My parents aren't home, but there's a letter on the table. I walk right past it. Only when I get out of the bathtub do I see that it's from Hana. I spend a long time drying my face with a washcloth. My hot skin itches, as if an electric current were buzzing through the air.

The letter takes me by surprise; I had completely forgotten about Hana. I remove a folded sheet covered in writing and can barely focus on it.

Two, three pages, an ordinary vacation letter. Swimming, the country house at Strakonice, colds, trips, mushroom picking. Do you already have your assignment done for September? Not me. Then I turn to the last page.

"And I also wanted to write you and say how much it bothers me that we ended what was a beautiful friendship. Maybe you already have another friend, but I still love you and will love you till I die."

All of it in tiny, perfectly formed handwriting, good enough for the American government. Just outside the window, lightning flashes. Fear instantly pins me to the wall. Scarcely a second later the thunder hits.

Sometimes it seems everything's just a fiction. A substitute for something that doesn't exist. In spite of this, each life has moments it can vouch for. This is one of them.

Outside it's pouring. In bed, flashlight in hand, I'm writing a letter. I love Hana so awfully much that there is no room for wonder. I didn't know it this morning, but now the whole past is nothing but a pedestal for my love. In the feeble glow of my flashlight, lines pour forth from me onto every page.

I love you. Till I die I will love only you. The mountain hurricane carries me through the air. Five pages spill, foaming, over the margins.

When I finish writing it is midnight. The house is asleep. I run along the balcony in the pouring rain and try to guess where Strakonice might be. Then I stand there in sheer triumph and project myself south-southwest. This is no fiction. It is no gesture. It is love itself. For it is high time the truth be told: if only I could experience such love again!

*

In the morning, Sasha is allowed outside. For the first time she roams the garden alone. I stay home, reading. Sometimes I peer out under the curtains and watch her wandering the paths. Only when I should be chopping carrots do I run out to see her.

"Hi. Were you sleeping?"

"No, why?"

" 'Cause you're later than usual."

"So?"

We sit, swinging our legs, on the edge of a basin full of wet branches. Sasha brushes lightly against my ankle.

"Are we going to play?"

"Play what?"

"The usual."

The sun makes a burning cap on my head. I twist my ankle around my other leg.

"I can't today."

"Why not?"

"I have a vacation assignment to do."

"An assignment? Over the summer?"

"Only the best students have to do them. Like me and my friend Hana."

Sasha kicks at the basin wall. A yellow powder drifts down from the crack.

"We both write pretty well. We wrote to President Eisenhower together."

"So then will you come down?"

"And we also wrote to the American government. To make sure there isn't a war. My friend has the prettiest handwriting in the whole class. And I do the best essays."

Sasha falls silent. Mr. Zámský comes trudging down the path. As soon as he spots us, he heads off. Suddenly a black spark of hatred flashes through me.

"Why do you keep kicking our wall?" I say. "You're going to wreck it!"

Sasha jumps down off the rim. I deliberately take my time picking bits of gravel out of the grass, but she doesn't turn around. I have to go home for lunch anyway.

Sasha left Prague two days later. We said a listless good-bye. Mr. Zámský left with her. I never sent the letter to Hana. I carried it around with me for a few days and then left it in the pocket of my windbreaker.

As for the Mountain of Mountains, Mount Everest got the furthest, but even he never made it to the summit. His transmitter went dead. He must have wiped away the snow and covered the frozen girl with his own body. Somewhere up there the trail disappears. No one has ever conquered the Mountain of Mountains.

In September Hana and I sit next to each other, but it's awkward and futile. The wheel of friendship doesn't spin round again. Fifth grade languidly and painlessly draws us apart.

One day I'm rushing down the hallway at school. There's a bulletin board there for the Young Communist Pioneers council. Suddenly something stops me in my tracks. "Dear President Eisenhower!" a tiny, familiar hand has written.

For a while I can't believe my eyes. Our letter has been in America for ages! After all, it was for President Eisenhower! Then finally the jolt hits me and in a flash I understand it all.

That letter was never intended to be sent. There was no hope it would reach its addressee; it was just pretend. It too was a gesture that missed its mark — a finger that might point somewhere, but somewhere it will never touch.

Boarskin Dances Down the Tables

The uneasy spirit of storytelling is forever glancing over its shoulder to see which slug-track, still slightly moist, we took to get where we are now. When I was sixteen, life brought me briefly into contact with a woman who could be my mother-in-law today, had that track led elsewhere. I had just run away from home after a major emotional storm and now I teetered at the very edge of my desire to survive it: I can still feel that almost intriguing sensation of vertigo. A fellow student offered me temporary asylum. Our relationship was unimportant. It was one of those brief, hazy bonds that leave behind only a shallow imprint, while what is essential (that segment of memory where the tidal wave incessantly pounds) is close at hand: in this instance, a spring morning when I'm weeding tulips with his mother. But more on that later.

I hesitate to mention the causes of that storm, lest I divert my attention from the matter at hand. So, just briefly: at home we had had what in espionage is called a *breach* — a sudden flood of information from a carefully guarded reservoir of knowledge. It happened when we breached my father's double life, which came complete with two apartments and two wives. He collapsed, sobbing piteously that he "couldn't have done otherwise, it was stronger" than him. My shocked heart had to choose. I could either judge him responsible and hate him — or accept that he truly could not have done otherwise, that life is always stronger than us and that all our plans are battles lost in advance. I plumped for the second version, threw my keys in the mailbox and ran away from home. But the spirit of storytelling lost interest in this a long time ago. What is this tale about, then? Well, for a start, it's about the word "taste."

My classmate's mother said I could call her Milada, but I never used her name and still think of her as Mrs. P.

Mrs. P. was over fifty and was a manager at a large savings bank. Her position carried significant responsibilities. Once I asked her what she did, and she said, "I work out savings plans for the following six-month period." I didn't understand this at all: was it really possible to plan an activity as random and absurdly capricious as the savings of thousands of unknown people? She smiled and said that it was.

Mr. P. was absent: the couple had divorced long ago and the husband had fled to parts unknown.

The son was predestined to devote his life to archaeology, which is what in fact happened. This plan too had been worked out by his mother. What lay behind it was not a romantic interest in the past, but rather an interest in the future, based on the annual reports of Charles University. The plan took into account a certain exclusivity (places were available only once every five years), the surprisingly low level of competition, and the field's considerable social prestige. When the boy was six, she started taking him to excavations instead of the zoo. He toddled along behind the archaeologists with a little shovel in his hand and an elegant mother at his side. In no time at all he became a sort of team mascot: a delightfully precocious little boy who was permitted to look at things up close and to document the day's finds with his bakelite camera.

Five years later Mrs. P.'s attention was caught by the neglected, empty display cases in the hallway of her son's school (she ran the Parents' Association). Through the boy, she ar-anged in them a quite decent exhibit on the history of Prague; there were even contributions from the Historical Institute of the Academy of Sciences, where mother and son were on friendly terms with a number of scholars. Mrs. P. alerted a television crew. Two representatives of the school spoke on the program: the principal and the boy. —Am I making myself clear? Need I add anything further to emphasize the theme that the spirit of storytelling has been moving toward all this time, a theme now manifest beneath the morass of facts? To the word "taste" I add the word "plan."

At the time I am speaking of, the mother concluded that to say "archaeology" was to say "Egypt" (we are on the threshold of the sixties; Mrs. P. knows what she is doing) and that acolytes familiar with Arabic would have a leg up. Through acquaintances she found an Arab dandy, a pudgy boy from an embassy, to converse with her son for an honorarium. Every other day, the room she had allotted me (they called it the "small salon") became a gateway to language. I refused to study Arabic, even though it was offered to me, and instead spent the time moping around pubs and indulging in feelings of futility.

⁂

It was precisely this volatile scent of futility that temporarily attracted the class nerd to me. For him, I had the sex appeal of heresy — which was, in truth, the only sex appeal I could muster. I was skinny, unkempt, pathetic. I was Boarskin. (We'll get to Boarskin shortly!) I was one of those girls to whom people say, "You know, you could look quite pretty if you only wanted to." Boarskin did not want to.

The sole thing keeping me alive was the strength of my resignation. I believed I wanted nothing from the world. A sullen prescience accompanied me, sensing *breaches* everywhere. Effort is pointless, the soul bereft. Something is forever lurking behind us, something stronger than our will; one day, all our plans will founder. And wanting to resist it is futile: underneath is an abyss of nothingness.

(A doodle in the margin: from the time he was a child, the boy had a sign hanging on the wall, which his mother had stenciled for him on drawing paper. It said: *Where there's a will, there's a way!* During puberty he had, in a moment of inspired insubordination, added a cartoon figure and the words: *Where there's a wind, watch which way you piss!* Both these contributions to the philosophy of will remained in place.)

The little man peeing into the wind and I: we were the only two escape attempts this exemplary boy ever made. The odds were about equal, that is, zero.

Mrs. P. had a hobby that took up a great deal of her time: Dutch tulips. She had a garden next to the house and, thanks to certain contacts abroad, a constant supply of the best quality bulbs. They came by express mail, in attractive plywood cartons, and were really from Holland.

The flower bed was enormous and planting it involved assiduous preparation. Every year Mrs. P. drew up new designs that resembled aerial maps. The blossoms bloomed according to plan and formed complicated ornaments, arranged with an eye to harmony of color and to the overall effect from both the windows and the street. The results were flawless, and she was rightfully proud of them. This hobby fit her perfectly: it was luxurious, but not provocatively so, it took effort (tulips were a lot of work) and, most of all, it was tasteful. And now it is time to shed light on the two words "Boarskin" and "taste."

Every day Mrs. P. — beige, calm, in practical low heels — walks through the "small salon" because there is no other way out of the house. I lie in bed in my tattered t-shirt, my dirty socks sticking out from under the pillow. I pretend to sleep and she quietly goes out. This moment completely saps my will to get up. The sixties are beginning and the word "taste" has a very special ring to it.

It is heard everywhere, it is the staunch protector of my childhood. You can dress tastefully or tastelessly. You dine tastefully, and entertain and decorate your home tastefully. Even art is primarily a matter of taste. Van Gogh is no longer crazy, but tasteful: he hangs in offices and dentists' waiting rooms, sanctified by the genial spirit of the times as an appropriate accessory. It is an era when my country has renounced religion and has adopted a notably nebulous moral codex. Taste is not a personal matter, it is a universal, a dogma, and certain forbidden combinations of colors (for example, "crazy to be seen in blue and green") have the taint of sin. It is as fixed as a nation's borders and as binding as grammar. There is taste and tastelessness: mixed states are rare, and decisions are quick as to whether the case in question (at this time, for example, the Beatles) belongs here, or there. There are people who are dependable in these matters, and Mrs. P. belongs among these elect few.

She fascinates me, and I cannot stand her. I flee from her any way I can. I roam aimlessly through empty Sundays, while she vacuums up the crumbs under my bed. A few times we clash in a fruitless debate and then steer clear of each other. Occasionally, when she is out, I walk through the apartment in envious indignation: everything in it harmonizes, like the music of the spheres. I have no taste; I cannot hear the secret voices that draw one thing to another. What's worse, I reject them. I proclaim chaos and nothingness, I say silly things, I bite my nails, even at the table, and loudly insist that taste is the jackboot of arrogant mediocrity. And beauty? No, I don't believe in beauty at all.

And now for the word "Boarskin."

A long time ago my school organized a children's fashion show aimed at developing our taste. For our edification and amusement (even humor was — in a certain restrained form — tasteful) they also offered an example to avoid. I was chosen for this heretical role: through the hazy layers of time I can see myself in stiletto heels swaying down the tables pushed together like a runway. I am in jeans and have a lacy jabot on my blouse, embodying what must be lunacy itself: after all, it is an unthinkable blunder, merely a cautionary exaggeration. In a few years this outfit will be commonplace, but today my classmates howl gleefully with laughter. There is music playing. I hop mink-like along the tables to its cha-cha rhythm, a stupid, saucy expression plastered deliberately across my face to emphasize the danger of my heresy. I am utterly intoxicated with my success. I still belong to the community of mankind. I am clear in my understanding of good and evil; the dogma is straightforward and transparent. What a simple spell! I am eleven.

A memory: I am six and the fairy tale about Boarskin is on the radio. Strangely uneasy, I bang my ruler against the table as I listen intently to the voice I am trying in vain to drown out. In that version she had a softer name: Mouse-Fur. I know her by other names, too: Donkey-Skin, Rag-Girl, Cap-o-Rushes, Leather-Dress, Catskin — but I usually think of her as Boarskin. Why? Of all the names, it is the nastiest.

In all these fairy tales a young girl, a princess, is so frightened by impending courtship that she flees her home. (Sometimes the theme is spiced with an incestual element: it is her own father who is courting her.) In a foreign land she conceals her beauty under an animal skin, blackens her face with ashes, and combs grease into her hair. Under the name Boarskin she takes shelter in the role of a mute farm-girl.

My stay at Mrs. P.'s marked the most extreme point of my Boarskin phase. I still instinctively avoid pictures of myself from that time, because my affliction was dirty and repulsive. My tattered and utterly unpoetic rags hung on me with none of the provocative charm of the hippies, who were to make their entrance later. I am not a flower child, I am a dirt child. I am a picture of a powerlessness that is not at all touching, of a resignation that healthy spirits avoid, and of a futility that is truly futile. There is no dirt under my nails, but only because I have bitten them to the quick.

It must be said that Mrs. P. accepted me quite generously as a "girl who'll grow out of it." She called my parents and told them I would be staying with her for a while and that it was all above board and respectable; she would not accept my meager savings. She tried at first to give me advice, but met with such obstinate resistance that she lapsed, relieved, into indifference — probably the truest feeling she had for me. I was there for just under three weeks; sometimes I cuddled passionlessly with her son, but I think that if anyone were to ask him today what he did that memorable spring, he would say, "I studied Arabic."

It is a hot, sunny morning in late April. The boy is having his lesson inside and we women are outside in the garden; in this sunshine I don't have the strength to wander the city alone. We are kneeling on the lawn, weeding the tulip bed: concentric circles of warm colors wave at the heavens. For once, there is no tension between us.

We chatter freely like women who till the soil, and Mrs. P. starts to open up. A certain colleague of hers at work, an older lady, has begun to act "oddly." Suddenly she does things that she never did before, that no one ever does. She rechecks figures — not only hers, but everyone else's too, which is not her responsibility; she is overstepping her authority, slowing the work down and, what's more, offending everyone. This comes at the expense of her own free time: she stays late at work, past dark, into the night, till midnight, and by now even twenty-four hours aren't enough for her utterly senseless tasks. Horrified at the thought that she might have overlooked a mistake somewhere, she takes taxis halfway across Prague to sit in the bank rechecking figures she had gone over earlier that day. She has begun to neglect herself: there is no time to change her clothes. Colleagues complain that she smells. One morning the custodian found her sobbing over a heap of scribbled papers, because all night long she hadn't been able to get the right results.

"If she won't give us some peace I'll have to reprimand her," Mrs. P. said, skillfully snipping a weed. "I hate to do it, but she's causing bad blood in the office."

"Reprimand her? When it's not her fault? After all, it's stronger than her!" I snap back, more loudly than I had intended. To my surprise, my throat constricts: from somewhere in that story the abyss looms up at me. I sense it and the weeder quivers in my fingers. Mrs. P. looks over, slightly startled, but with a firm hand immediately turns the clay over again.

"You think so?" she says evenly. "You know, I believe she's doing it on purpose. With a bit of effort, she wouldn't do such silly things. After all, any reasonable person can see she's being silly, don't you think?"

For a moment I am motionless, but the weeder still shivers. I almost can't believe my ears: for the next thirty years I will hear those words float through the warm morning, how peaceful they sound in the spring breeze.

Before me is a woman who has lived more than half a century. She has raised a son, managed a bank. She has proved her prowess at living and surviving; she is among those who determine the world's tastes. And yet to her, madness is deliberate silliness, peeing impudently into the wind. Just "a bit of effort" and you can change your ways.

I dig my fingers into the soil and close my eyes. My tongue clings to my mouth like a stuck zipper. Hot, dense anger rises inside me; it washes over me like blinding sea-spray. In that sentence is everything I am trying to escape: the godlike arrogance of people with no doubts. The joviality of eyewitnesses to a catastrophe, the unfeeling righteousness of those who are sure of their figures, and that eternal, smoothly ironed serenity! Must I admit that at the root of my grumbling is envy? My entire will to tell stories springs from it — and it's now been (alas!) thirty years.

Finally I open my eyes and Mrs. P. glances at me encouragingly. The soft spring air floats on the breeze. And as sometimes happens to that scale inside us, the cramp of anger slackens and is replaced by sorrow, until it melts my bones and there is nothing in my field of vision but flowers. The morning sun shines through the tulips, its light gushes through the living tissue of petals. It is like an unexpected blow; I have no chance to resist their beauty. I burst into tears (for the first time since the *breach*) and flee headlong from yet another home.

And so I ended my strange visit, and the life of Mrs. P. and her son went on without me for another thirty years.

The times themselves changed markedly. The word "taste" faded and retreated to the twilight of speech: the era of its supremacy is past. I must say that I regret this a little, but the dogma of those I share my life with says that taste is a haughty hoax. The buoys that warned swimmers have long since been dashed against the cliff.

At sixteen I voted defiantly for chaos. As I grow older, I long for an orderly foundation to cling to; I pray for an easy repose and I simplify my life as much as I can. Sometimes I dream of that classroom from my childhood, but I am no longer prancing down the runway like a freak; I am sitting in the anonymous pack below, roaring with laughter like the others, falling in a heap from our chairs. We are inside, laughing without rancor at those on the outside: crazy accountants, Boarskins, traitorous fathers. Outside, I know, is the abyss — and for almost half a century I have lived so adroitly that I have not ended up in it.

It was half coincidence that led me back to Mrs. P. thirty years later, and half the gravitational pull of my own tracks. Mrs. P. had hardly changed at all: I found her perfectly coiffed and the apartment spotless, as if I'd left only yesterday. She remembered who I was, and took me into the salon, which was just the same as before.

"You look good," she offered — for my Boarskin days were behind me. Now my main ambition is to blend into the background.

"Thank you," I answered. "I hear you have a famous son. You must be glad he's done so well."

Mrs. P. looked straight at me. "I have no son," she said firmly. I did not understand. I had seen him that very day on television; he had been chairing a conference. I recognized him mostly by his resemblance to his mother, not because he had stuck so firmly in my memory.

"For me, my son has ceased to exist," she continued without a quiver, "because he's rejected me. He has his own life, and there is no room for me in it, because he doesn't need me anymore. But I've forgotten about him too. Supposedly he has children — I don't know, that's what people have told me. He moved out and I'm not interested in where he's living now. Let's not talk about him anymore. I'll make you some tea."

And in fact we did not talk about him again. We exchanged banalities, and her unflappability fascinated me as deeply as before. Nothing, not a hair, not a speck of dust on the table, betrayed what a terrible trick life had played on her. I could only admire her: she had survived the defeat of her own will, her greatest plan had failed completely — but she did not let herself be defeated. She did not permit her doubts to gnaw at her. At eighty she was even more steadfast than before.

When Mrs. P. went to cut us some strudel, I absent-mindedly walked over to the window. What I saw took my breath away.

It was the height of spring; the tulips were in their full glory. In the middle of them, right in the middle of the flowers, swayed a pair of plastic bags with tomato plants in them. The tulip bed had resembled concentric circles. Now a sparse potato patch spilled into them, and from beneath its plants spurted an overgrown caraway, burnt by the sun. Beans wound their way up rusty pipes. There were no plots or rows, just the painfully offensive chaos of plants strangling one another.

At first I thought it might be a mistake; it was far too impossible. Certain things simply are not done, not even in this strange time, when no one asks what's allowed. The dogma has fallen, water has covered the weir of taste — but still it was hard to imagine what impulse could possibly induce anyone to plant potatoes next to tulips! It wasn't for lack of space — all around were swards of grass large enough for all her vegetables. It looked grotesque. Only madness itself could reject all limits this way. It was a *breach*. Beyond the fence lay a motley bed of despair.

Mrs. P. came in with a tray. I quickly averted my eyes from the window. We then had a smooth conversation about nothing.

"By the way, what happened to that lady, you know, the one who kept rechecking figures?" I asked in the vestibule, with one foot already out the door. Mrs. P. wrinkled her forehead.

"One moment," she said, recollecting. "Aha, I know. She slit her wrists," she said matter-of-factly. "Why do you ask?"

I shrugged. She handed me my coat. She did not invite me back and I did not say I'd come again.

I was on my way out when Mrs. P. suddenly smiled.

"I just remembered something!"

The pleasant memory made her face grow younger.

"You know, she was here once. She fell in love with my tulips. Couldn't get enough of them. She was an exceedingly strange woman, but she did have taste."

Far and Near

I switched on the television and instantly we were face to face again. A man I had not seen in twice-seven biblical years stared straight into my eyes and spoke to me urgently. Between us was the screen's one-way mirror, which shielded me perfectly. For a moment there was no sound and I could not understand his words. It was perfect déjà vu.

The show was some sort of panel discussion about science fiction, and my long-lost friend — a literary critic, incidentally — was speaking about the leitmotif of "far and near" and about various resolutions of it which this genre had offered. Distance, he opined, is not a physical fact, but primarily a state of mind.

"If I have the gate key," he said in the same deep but flat voice that had once instructed me, "then only an insignificant layer of wire mesh separates me from the garden. If I do not have it, I have to go around to the back of the house, cross the construction site, slip past the shed, and go down the steps."

This example was especially apt, because I knew exactly which gate (site, shed, steps) he meant. It was my gate, my garden.

It was a large television screen and they had zoomed in on his face. We were just as close as we'd been before.

This will be a story about the far and the near. It is not science fiction and will offer no new resolutions.

*

When I was twenty-two, a serious young man appeared in my life. He was probably thirty — I don't know, I didn't ask. At the time, he was a columnist for one of the cultural reviews and had read my stories somewhere. We met in a café.

From the very first moment, I was struck by a certain contradiction. He was reserved and abstract like no man I had ever known. He seemed absolutely unapproachable. And yet he sat closer to me than even the liveliest of them. He did not touch me. Not once that evening did he even try for a single accidental contact as he explained things in a slow, earnest manner with his face right up next to mine.

I listened with only half an ear, because he made me feel strangely insecure. I cannot remember anything from that first meeting besides the awkward feeling that he was making a detailed, mirthless examination of my wrinkles and pores, of my irregular blotch of rouge, speaking all the while with languid fervor about sentence structure in the postwar short story.

Through the windows Prague swam in a murky twilight. A dark pink band hung over the horizon like a scarf carried skyward.

"The short stories I like best are those I understand least," he said. "And of those, I prefer the ones I don't get till years after I read them."

He didn't mention any by name, but he was not talking about mine, which tried to be enigmatic, but were as transparent as an aquarium and nearly as deep.

The duality of his signals perplexed me. This man, as psychotherapy would say, entered other people's bubbles. He did not respect that invisible membrane — *noli me tangere,* the circle drawn round us with consecrated chalk. The space freezes. Only a whirling tremble divides us, one that knows full well what it is doing. It admits only love and aggression. When lovers and brawlers embrace, it opens wide like a door on a sensor, letting the intruder inside. Everyone's bubble is a different size. Mine is just big enough. I can't stand claps on the shoulder, indiscriminate familiarity, or confidences. I sit in my bubble — rather satisfied, a little hostile, and self-possessed.

Dr. M., as I called him, also seemed rather satisfied, a little hostile, and most of all self-possessed. His self-possession was as rigid as an inflated plastic bag. It was remarkably rare to see him smile. He never confided anything. I remember well his personal scent: he smelled like toothpaste. Dr. M. was always meticulously clean; the only thing disturbing the impression that he had just rolled out of a car wash was the dark pink band across his forehead, some sort of birthmark.

For one brief moment we reached the threshold of love, but it brought us no closer. We never dropped the formalities. He did not have the key to my garden.

After that first time, we began to meet sporadically and — as I would call it today — exchange brain outputs. We were two reviewers conversing. No one reading a stenographic record of our meetings would see in them a young man and woman. His indifference would have suited me perfectly (at a time when I was strangely deaf to the world of emotions, when my immature and unengaged heart felt as tough as a turnip), were it not for that violent familiarity perpetrated on my bubble.

Boundaries create plotlines. Border skirmishes and balk plowing provide the fuel of history. Limits in space and time are literary stimuli.

"Today's prose is nothing but monologue," he was saying. "Its growing incomprehensibility springs not from any formal characteristics, but rather from a fundamental resignation to its failure to be understood. The author does not want to be understood, because he does not even understand himself. He is showing us that comprehension is impossible. The omniscient author is passé. This century has realized that knowledge always comes too late. It resolves nothing and does not protect mankind from anything."

As he spoke, he leaned over so close that my bubble, in a panicky defense, shot off an electrostatic charge, arced across and clung to his face like a death mask made of freezer wrap.

"We're wrong," he said with unusual gravity. "We're not ourselves, we're not in ourselves, and we're never where we ought to be."

I'd already ruled out the possibility that he was hard of hearing. On the contrary, he had sensitive hi-fi ears, and more than once we exchanged a noisy pub for a cocoon of quiet, for the empty corners of exceedingly vile bistros, and there conducted our lethargic, wobbly, pointless conversations, at a safe distance from anything that could touch us. What did we talk about? About "archetypal natural settings." About "mythical elements of reality." About "the profanization of the leitmotif of coincidence and of any defining moment." About things that exist and do not exist, and whose pale veins teem with paper blood.

It was — it should have, would have, could have been — a happy sexless nothing. Two hermaphroditic brains floated in a solution of irresponsibility: ageless, outside reality, without a future. If only we had not been so tinglingly close to each other that our auras' furs bristled with crackling violet sparks.

He had the unmistakable imago of a bachelor: a narrow-gauge intellectual sense of humor, his screws sunk tight. He was married but never spoke of his wife, except in passing ("I'll be away, but my wife will send it to me."). I learned somewhere that she was an anesthesiologist, substantially older than him, and apparently very beautiful. I didn't think about her, beautiful or not.

We met more and more often, practically every day. He began to walk me home (garden, site, shed, steps), but otherwise our meetings were no different from before, except maybe for a certain facility. We skipped a step in our development. In half a year we were an aging married couple, with his indifferent faithfulness and weary sensuality. He would wait for me at the university. We would go to movies or exhibits. Everyone believed we were lovers, but we only listened to each other with half an ear and were no closer than two stuffed lizards.

Sometimes it seemed to me that everything was already behind us: sobs of passion, rampages, dragging each other by the hair. That it had happened long ago, in some other time that we had already forgotten. We were an old couple on a look-out tower. The world lay far below us; the bare, distant trees stuck up from the horizon like spikelets on a blade of wheat.

Twice in my life there have been times when the whole world of feelings, with its demonic dankness, has seemed incomprehensibly foreign to me, artificial to its very core, affected and cloying. The first time, I was ten: romance novels enticed me into an exuberant arrogance and a know-it-all cheerfulness. The second was now: without knowing why, I had escaped the force field of love for a year or two, and its vibrations did not pass through me. Maybe a third will soon be upon me, and this time it will last. Certainly our friendship, if you can call it that, was the best thing I could have wished for. It freed me from the opprobrious stigma of solitude. Concepts and phrases formed a haze around us. Thanks to them, I was at peace, and I did not have to dance the tortuous courtship dances of my age. Only I never did see how Dr. M. profited from this strange relationship.

*

Before Christmas we casually said our good-byes, exchanged presents (books for books, of course), and set a meeting for January. We were such strangers to each other that neither thought to ask how the other was spending the holidays. I stayed at home with my parents and then set off to Budapest for a New Year's Eve concert.

The train chugged across a flat, charmless landscape; heaps of thawing snow dotted the fields like sour cream. I dozed for part of the night, and woke to the slanted rays of the early morning sun. The train cars were divided into rows with two seats each. In the sharp, immature light of daybreak I saw a singular woman sitting across the aisle from me. I hadn't noticed her before.

She had the classic profile and indeterminate age of a beauty bred in the bone; she could have been anywhere from thirty to fifty. A knot of hair, jet black, and a guarded face too carefully made up. She gave the impression she had not slept at all, but had kept watch all night, staring intently into the dark. Directors classify all female roles as blondes or brunettes. And they don't mean hair color. Everyone understands what they mean. Ophelia is blonde, like vanilla pudding. Lady Macbeth is nothing if not brunette.

I took her for a Hungarian. Not only because of her hair — it was more her air of foreignness: addressing her in Czech was out of the question. Addressing her at all was out of the question. Her bubble was like a concrete shelter.

When I spotted her, she had just begun to remove the rings on her long, pale fingers. She had advertising hands; her nails were traffic-light red. Slowly, with single-minded attentiveness, she took off ring after ring (there were seven of them, one a wedding band), carefully laid them aside on the fold-down tray, and then slowly and thoroughly began to rub an expensive, artificial-smelling cream into her hands. The procedure was an unusually long one, and the woman stared at her hands the whole time like a surgeon during an operation.

This spectacle fascinated me. By itself it was ordinary: there was nothing special about a woman putting lotion on her hands in the morning. But there was something strange in her tenacity. She set the cream aside and put the seven rings back on. She did not look around or glance out the window. For a while she sat and stretched her fingers. Then she removed her rings again, this time in anxious haste, set them on the tray and applied another dose. She rubbed in the cream, grinding one hand against the other. Her knuckles were white. Her face remained impassive as she wrung her hands in a gesture of utmost despair.

Suddenly the man next to her stood up; I had not noticed him before over the high divider between their seats. He stepped over her legs without a word, and because the tray further narrowed the already impassable gap between her and the seatback in front, he had to press his whole body against her. He did not look at her, nor she at him. She did not even symbolically move her legs aside to show that she wanted to make way for him, and he did not make the slightest effort to pass more considerately. There was no apology for entering each other's bubbles. He overcame her like a geographical obstacle; she went on moisturizing her hands. They were from different universes where different laws applied. It looked terribly rude, even though nothing had happened. But there was a warning of sorts in that mutual disregard. It was a banal moment, but a defining one as well; there was a mute, lurking evil about it. The man worked his way through to the aisle and walked quickly toward the dining car. He did not notice me. It was Dr. M.

The woman's face gave nothing away. She recapped the cream and put on her seven lures of beauty. The wedding band was the one I knew from his hand. I vanished, resettling three cars down, and once in Budapest I took great care not to meet them, even by accident.

*

In January we met as usual. The incident on the train had taken root in my mind. I did not understand it, nor did I want to. I wanted to have a companion to protect me from the outside world, but one without any rights — like a folding screen.

Prague was completely socked in that winter. It was pretty side up; the tattered, dirty obverse stayed face down. We were returning from a movie, walking quite exceptionally arm in arm across the expanse of snow. It was that twilight hour, when everything is suspended. The snow had the crunch of a freshly created world. Suddenly, unbelievably, from out of nowhere came the smell of violets.

Mythical elements of reality! Archetypal natural settings! We cannot escape them; there is no way out. The emotion at the heart of those twilight winter moments: the lively hush of whirling snow, the nearness of a warm, foreign body. A lyrical drumstroke, when amid the frost and the dwindling light, the scent of spring flickers past like a flying carpet.

The veil of snowflakes parted; a lanky boy stood in front of us in a rather flimsy coat for such a cold winter, a thicket of tangled, rust-colored curls hanging down past his ears.

"Hi!" he said to me, and then smiled radiantly. We had never seen each other before. M. pressed me a bit closer to himself.

"So this is her?" the youth continued, this time to M., but without taking his eyes off me. "The writer?"

"What are you doing here?" Dr. M. replied evasively. He sounded strange: as if he were carrying a tray of delicate, long-stemmed wineglasses, putting one foot carefully in front of the other. "I thought you weren't here. You promised you'd be gone."

"I was waiting for my tram on Peace Square. I was just about to get on when the Holy Spirit stepped on my foot. So I guess I'm supposed to be right here. I told you, I let myself be guided."

"What do you mean, on Peace Square? You were supposed to be out in the bush long ago."

"Guess not, if I'm here."

Again he gave me a conspiratorial smile. "He doesn't believe I'm guided. Still doesn't want to believe me. I'm always in the right place. Exactly where he needs me at that very moment. Like those avalanche dogs."

"Look, we're in a bit of a hurry."

We were not in a hurry. All three of us knew that no one was in a hurry. The kid did not have the generosity to let it pass, and gave a grimace of indulgent disbelief.

"He's lying," he pointed out chummily to me, "and he has no reason to. He couldn't even explain why he's lying. He thinks I'm his adversary, some sort of antipodean. But he's the antipodean. Except he doesn't want to admit it. It's the anesthesia, I think. Most of the time he's under anesthesia. Right?"

Ropes of steam, imbued with their own independent lives, flowed from their mouths and twined about each other long after the sound of their words had died away. Dr. M. grew more and more nervous. Through the layers of our sleeves I felt his arm instinctively pulling me away, but his feet stood obstinately still as if this odd conversation would last into the night. The boy suddenly pulled out a crumpled band with a door key hanging from it.

"I'll take your measure." He glanced at me encouragingly, as if he were promising me some sort of fun. "I'll measure your writer," he informed Dr. M. "You know I'm never wrong."

It was like a dream. An archetypal setting: the deepening darkness and the deepening whiteness of the snow, the hot clump of violets in the frost, the illusion of isolation on an island, while around its borders anonymous shadows glided past — all of this gave the episode a sort of latent, cryptogamous meaning, a plot invested for future interest. Violets: the boy had a woven sachet of herbs around his bare neck. Snowflakes melted on his rusty curls. He approached me, took my hand unaffectedly, turned it palm up, and started to swing the key above it.

"Don't be afraid," he said sweetly. "The Holy Spirit guides me. I don't hurt anyone."

The key, suspended from between his pinky and thumb, slowly began to sway. Transfixed, I watched the gradually increasing motion, which truly seemed to flow from some source outside the youth's will. Not even his fingers moved, but the key gyrated ever more wildly, till it was whirling like a dervish in ecstasy.

"She's okay," the boy pronounced confidently. He licked the key on both sides and then squeezed it between his palms. "With time she'll get better. But not for you."

"That's enough," Dr. M. answered in a level, expressionless tone. "We have to go."

The boy simply ignored this news. Again his fingers lowered the key; it came to life and fidgeted restlessly, like a horse pawing with its hoof.

"Release her!" he ordered sharply. M.'s arm grudgingly loosened. The key flew here and there for a while and then — as if it had found its trajectory — began to swing sharply between us like a pendulum.

"You see?" the youth said amiably. "Tuck in your forewings. This writer isn't for you."

He stopped the key and turned my way, looking me right in the eye, the way most people never do. Despite the absurdity and disjointedness of the whole situation, he was so nonchalant that he did not come across as frightening or intrusive.

"He's not the one," he announced confidentially. He unbuttoned the doctor's coat and cheerfully tapped a finger against the man's chest.

"Anyone there?"

M. just stared past his shoulder. The streetlamps flared to life and a cone of light fell down on us as on a stage.

"You see?" the boy said. "He's not there. But where is he? He's afraid of what's inside, because he has an evil sprite in his heart. He's fine, really, but the sprite keeps giving him bad advice. My advice is good, but what can I do when he's not here? And when he is, he's under anesthesia. That's so he can pretend he doesn't hear me."

He glanced at the key, placed it on his palm, and stuck out his hand. The way people give presents to small children. For a moment time stopped or, at least, slowed to an imperceptible crawl. Everything stood stock still, the snow paused in its fall. Then M. took the key and put it in his pocket. The pink band on his forehead sparkled with frost. The boy laughed softly and ran off down the street. The rusty tuft of hair quickly dissolved into the snowy darkness.

*

Invisible violets, a dancing key, an evil sprite in his heart. Mythical elements in the logic of fact. This is the logic of fact, at least the logic of biased memory.

When the youth left us, we walked off quickly, without a word. We no longer walked arm in arm. Since we often did not talk on our strolls, today we could easily conceal what we were so stubbornly silent about. Cold and confusion were battling within me. A fit of shivering came over me, and I wanted to be home as soon as possible. The moment of twilight had passed, the snow had stopped falling, and a bare winter darkness had descended.

At the gate I found I did not have my keys. There was no point in ringing the bell of an empty house, but there was the aforementioned route past the construction site.

"Just so I know you're home safe," he mumbled, and we stumbled through the dark over the frozen planks, the tattered cardboard, and the frozen, desolate disorder of the abandoned lot. I clenched my teeth firmly so they wouldn't chatter, and my face hardened into an obdurate expression of defiance and pique.

We ended up at the cellar door. I had my hand on the icy doorknob.

"You wouldn't marry me," he said suddenly, without a question mark, rhythmless, in the flat tone of an inconsequential statement. I was cold. I didn't want to know anything, didn't want to make any decisions. My bubble stiffened with frost and would not let the news inside.

"No," I said, just as unemphatically. It was a reaction right from my spinal cord, a simple reflexive arc that bypassed my brain. I did not know why I said it. It was not a genuine question, nor a genuine answer.

M. nodded slightly, then symbolically raised a finger to his cap and left. I did not wait for him to disappear from view. Inside I found the gate key fallen into a fold in my bag.

*

That night I had a dream, I believe the first one that had ever featured M. I am at the railway station in Budapest. The dream, as if focusing in on its core, rushes through several episodes until suddenly I see the empty trackyard. Dr. M. is walking along a track, tie after tie, on his hands. He has an ecstatic expression, one I've never seen on him, and in his eyes is the dull gleam of madness. He says something, implores me deeply, with a visionary's emphasis on every word, except that I understand nothing. I run along the track, trying with all my strength to understand, but in vain: I hear his voice and his words make no sense. Then a train emerges from beneath the horizon.

With this the dream takes on a tinge of terror, and of terribly ruinous responsibility. The train comes nearer, M. is still unaware of it and continues speaking in a feverish rapture. Rising through me is a sheer, violent whirlwind of horror and love, a jet from the bottomless absolute, beyond all imagination; destruction hurtles closer and closer until in a panic I shout out two words. The words are: "I know!"

I don't know what I know. I don't know in my dreams, nor when I'm awake, but I must say it because it is the only way I can avert the catastrophe: everything depends on my knowing something. Except it's too late, or my knowledge is too weak:

the dream answers with a dreadful clash of matter. My own scream awakens me, I am gripped by a raging fever and an all-engulfing sense of powerlessness.

Since that moment twice-seven years have passed. I am thirty-seven, married for the second time. I am sure that my life never had and will never again have a greater intensity than at the moment of that scream. No bliss or distress has ever seized me that way. In concentric and ever widening circles various bliss-tresses revolve around me, but they weigh less. No one has ever been nearer to me.

Dr. M. never called again. I did not understand. I did not know what had happened to him; I was utterly perplexed. For some reason I couldn't feel any pain; it was more a loss of the earth beneath my feet, a vacuum devoid of all coordinates. I wasn't lonely, I didn't miss him, but I could not get rid of him. His absence was just a different sort of presence, like when you know that an uninvited guest has fallen asleep outside your door. I did not search for him. There or not, he became an oppressive phantom, pushing against my bubble from the outside.

Shortly thereafter I met my first husband, we emigrated, and time — for a time — took on a different theme. I heard nothing of M. I married again, had two children. I returned to Bohemia. The wind erased my tracks. Fourteen years on, I flew off to Brisbane, in Australia, to a congress on contemporary literature.

Fresh jet lag raged within me: two giant airplanes had overtaken time by nine hours. They had thrown me into the near future: in Brisbane it was a summer afternoon, while in me the Czech winter night rushed toward morning. I wasn't sick, the way they had warned me, but I had the confused feeling that I wasn't here. My wakefulness was uneasy and my body slept a narcotic sleep. I had to watch where my hand was and direct it with my sight, as if by remote control; otherwise I would miss my sleeve. As if I were not where I was.

At the hotel I took a shower and walked into the bedroom. My roommate, a Czech emigré, was sitting on the desk, shaving her legs. So as not to watch, I switched on the television — and instantly we were face to face again. He stared at me from the screen. He was here and not here, as always. The sound was on low and he was speaking English. For a moment I couldn't understand a word. He was lecturing on the far and the near. He mentioned a "wicket," but he meant a gate, my gate, my garden.

"What program is this?" I asked the girl.

"It's a video from last year's conference. It's on in all the rooms."

She looked over: "That guy's Czech, coincidentally. He caused a real scene here a few years back."

She mowed one of her strong calves with her razor.

"Supposedly he'd been cheating on his wife back in Prague. The lady hopped on the first plane, gun in hand. She got into the hotel, then somehow snuck into his room and — splat! Except clearly she couldn't even see straight. Her traitor wasn't in. An unfortunate coincidence, she'd shot someone else ... but who?"

Buzzing razor in hand, she stared off into the distance.

"Yeah! The hotel waiter, that red-headed klutz. Poor guy, just walked blindly into it. Well, there are people like that: always in the wrong place."

Disparagingly, she tapped the razor against her forehead.

"And then she turned and shot herself. Must have been nuts."

That news had been looking for me for fourteen years. It found me in Brisbane, Australia, on the top floor of the Space Hotel. Its traveling speed was four kilometers a day. Straggling like a blind turtle toward the intersection of time and space, it was fourteen years late and nine hours ahead. So now I knew, and what use was it to me? It didn't concern me yet — or anymore. Two times passed each other inside me like overlapping transparencies on a screen.

"What's wrong? Jet lag?" said the antipodean with good-humored sympathy, buzzing her razor past my nose. "Do I ever know! I'm always flying somewhere and it totally messes me up. It's like you're not here," she pointed to her chest, "you don't care about anything. People speak, I hear them, but I still don't know what they're saying."

"I know," I said mechanically. And then once more: "I know."

Two Revolts in One Family

The son, Jan — for unknown reasons called Iša at home — rebelled against his mother's omnipotence only once, when he was sixteen. He spent a week planning his escape from home. In the gray of early morning he snuck out to the highway to hitch a ride. His luck was unprecedented. The third vehicle to come along picked him up and took him to a remarkable place, Paseky: with its deserted mountain meadows, it was the ideal hideout for a runaway. The driver, a chatty, jolly butterball of a man, even pointed him to a wooden hut, where they let him stay in return for a bit of work. It was a fabulous success. Iša spent August at the old shepherd's, becoming quite decent with a scythe and as bronzed as an Indian.

When he returned home a day before the end of the holidays, all his mother said was: "Hello." And after a pause: "Your messages are on your door." Iša went to read his messages, which she had been taking all month with the precision of a perfect secretary, and from that moment on he never rebelled again.

The daughter, Eva, three years older, spent her entire life rebelling against her mother. She turned her adolescence into an unending diatribe against this and that, constantly reasoning with her mother: in the first place, the second, the third, the fourth. Eva was almost always right. But in the end things went the way her mother wanted.

The fact was, her mother was "very good with people." Throughout Eva's childhood her mother told her: "You have to know what works with whom. Let people be right, and then do things your own way." Her daughter swore that she would never take after her mother. She would not scheme, she would be true and brutal and straightforward: at forty Eva had three divorces behind her. "Love without absolute openness is deception!" she would argue. Her mother would just smile slightly: "Of course, Eva darling."

Now they were all sitting at the table, because Eva had insisted on a family meeting. The problem was that Father, who at seventy had just survived a second heart attack, had decided to "rip down Malšov" over the summer; that is, to renovate their holiday cottage in the village of Malšov, which meant getting rid of the old roof, putting up a new one, and then replastering the entire place.

"It's ludicrous!" Eva shouted, but she shouted quietly, because Father was sleeping in the next room; the shout sounded like it was out of a radio play. "Dad shouldn't even pick up a garbage can! Do you understand what a second heart attack is? Do you have any idea what it means to have a heart attack? And in less than a month you're sending him to rip down a house!"

"But Eva darling," her mother said soothingly, "Dad's a reasonable fellow. He won't be ripping anything down. He'll find himself a nice comfy seat in the shade and direct the Šefl boys. He won't have to lift a finger."

"For Christ's sake, Mom, open your eyes! Come on, Iša! Don't just sit there like a pasty-faced statue! At least say something clever! As if Dad will stand by and watch other people work! An hour of that and he'll be carting bricks and climbing around the roof like a monkey!"

Iša, who had long since lost the muscles developed when he ran away, sat hunched over, with his thinning pate visible. He was carefully making a design out of matches on the tablecloth. His nails were short, as those of a child who bites them. The expression on his face was what Eva called "the unhappily married old young man."

"If Mother thinks Dad's up to it, then he's up to it," he said, annoyed. Eva drummed her fingers on the table.

"Then listen up, boy! In the first place! Dad's doing Malšov for us, in case you hadn't realized! For us, since we're both so incompetent we can't even pull out the bathtub stopper. He's in a hurry. Know why? Because he's afraid he'll die, and that we're such numbskulls we'll let the cottage slowly collapse around us. He's willing to kill himself for us! The doctor said—"

"Doctors overdramatize things, Eva," her mother's voice unexpectedly broke in. "A bit of exercise in the fresh air will only help him."

Eva groaned inside. It's always the same, still the same old powerlessness, and not even twenty years and three marriages have made her any stronger. She's banging her head against a wall. She's right, it goes without saying, but her mother's impervious affability wins the day again.

"Mom!" she said beseechingly. "Don't be blind! It's suicide! Dad's worked himself to death, he's an old man, his heart has given out twice already, and I simply won't permit—"

At that moment the door opened and their father stood there, having only had twenty of his winks.

"What's the big discussion?" he said sleepily. He looked like a large, flaccid bear. His pyjamas hung on him like a flag on a still day. Mother smiled indulgently.

“Eva’s just afraid Malšov will be too much for you. Except it won’t happen without you. You can’t leave Šefl alone with it. He’s a nice fellow, but you have to tell him everything twice. And he’s really not the builder you are.”

Dad’s not a builder! Dad’s a retired foreman! God, is she slick! How did she give him the illusion he wore the pants in the family? Eva’s heart almost burst with tenderness for this easily deceived man. It was up to her. She was the only one with the courage to face the truth — the truth that this was a matter of life and death.

Her father gave a weak but delighted smile.

“Well, true. If I don’t take the roof down, it’ll come down on its own,” he said genially.

The night after this family assembly was a filter, trapping all the defeats and losses of forty years. Eva would wake up, then fall back to sleep again. At a feverish clip she dreamed up plan after plan, each more hopeless than the last, including blowing the cottage to smithereens. Finally — on the narrow threshold of daybreak — she decided to revolt.

Could no one see that her mother was losing her mind? Did her cobra-like will hypnotize them so completely? It wasn’t will, it was loss of judgment in old age! But no one in this clan sees anything they don’t want to see. In the weak light of dawn Eva sat on the bed, shaking her head over all these people hopelessly afflicted with blindness.

The plan that emerged from the detritus of many other plans was simple. Tomorrow she would set out for Mr. Šefl’s in Malšov. She would fall on her knees before him, metaphorically of course, but she must be careful not to reason with him. No fancy talk with Mr. Šefl. What got to him was emotion.

She imagined herself bursting into tears and saying: "Mr. Šefl, you're my only hope! Please consider my father's heart!" (No, even better: "Save my dad!") "If you go ahead with Malšov, it will be on your conscience. Think of an excuse. Your back's acting up, for instance. Or you can't get the wood. Whatever, for God's sake, Dad won't start without you."

She hoped she'd be able to cry for real. Her mother would manage it easily. Once Eva had asked her how she was able to cry at will. Her mother had said: "You know, child, it's not that hard. You just have to throw yourself into it."

The second part of the plan, of course, was to convince Mr. Šefl not to breathe a word to her mother. This was the hard part, for Mr. Šefl — like all men, incidentally — thought her mother was a very pleasant lady. If her mother followed Eva's tracks and tried to pooh-pooh her concerns, she'd wrap Šefl around her little finger and Eva's guerilla tactics would come to nothing.

Oddly, the knowledge that at forty she was going behind her mother's back for the first time both disheartened and exhilarated her. She had built her life on a tactlessness bordering on the passionate. Having pledged herself to a life of virtue and confrontation, here she was, plotting this naive intrigue.

I have the right, she said to herself. I have the right and the responsibility. Forty years of subservience is enough. It is time to change the guard, it occurred to her, and she instantly fell into a vivid dream.

She was nineteen and chasing Iša around Malšov. She wanted to protect him, although she wasn't exactly sure from what. "Run away, you chicken! Go on, run! Why did you come back, chicken!" she shouted at him, just like she used to. Suddenly her brother turned to her. The expression on his face amazed her. He was happy: deliriously, magnificently happy, as she had never been.

There was no direct connection to Malšov, so she had to change buses three times, reaching the village at nine that evening. Sleepy, battered, with the taste of some revolting cookie in her mouth, she pounded on the window.

But the moment she entered, she wanted to take to her heels. The Šefls' kitchen was full. A wheezy woman was mixing dough, three fellows were guzzling caraway brandy, and a fat, unfamiliar child was sitting on the floor, shaving bits of colored pencil right onto the floor.

Eva wilted. In her nighttime fantasies she had spoken with Mr. Šefl alone; her heartrending outburst was directed only at him. It had not occurred to her that half of Malšov would be present. And she knew no one would leave. There was no room for intrigues in the village; people here lived openly and out loud. This was, incidentally, what she had always dreamed of. Two of her marriages foundered on her attempt to turn their home into a brightly lit stage.

"Well I'll be! Young lady!" Mr. Šefl hollered. Eva could smell his brandy across the room. "What in God's name brings you here?"

The noise in the kitchen stopped instantly. Everyone turned toward Eva. She had to summon all her strength even to cross the threshold.

"Got something nice for us, young lady?"

The woman with the bowl of dough was breathing heavily. The child ran its pencil over Eva's ankle. The other five people looked her over with undisguised interest. The muscles around Eva's mouth tightened.

"I see I've come at a bad time," she said too rapidly and, for some reason, a bit defensively. A speck of dirt had gotten behind her contact lens and now was not a good time to take it out. Just get it over with, she advised herself, and continued even more curtly.

"Don't worry, I don't mean to bother you. I'm here on account of my father. You couldn't have known, but he's in serious shape. In the first place, he's seventy, and in the second, he's just had another heart attack."

I'm reasoning with him, I'm reasoning again! She felt a wave of despair. I sound like a Martian. I wanted to be simple and touching, I wanted to cry. The dust speck behind her lens made her scrunch her eyelid curiously. Her eye was suffering, like an oyster making a pearl. Eva took a deep breath.

"Mr. Šefl, you're supposed to do that roof for my father."

She caught sight of his wife, a pair of chicken shears in her hand, listening inhospitably. The child was poking her in the leg with the pencil point.

"Mr. Šefl, it's out of the question. Absolutely out of the question. I have to ask you not to take the job."

The silence in the room thickened. Everyone, even the child with the pencil, was staring at her blankly. Unintentionally she tensed her calves and fell to her knees. She had the unhappy feeling that it was a losing cause.

"But young lady," Mr. Šefl said with surprise in his voice, "it's all worked out, isn't it? I thought you knew. Your mother was here about two weeks ago, and asked me to beg off the roof. She cried, the poor thing, did she ever cry! She was afraid your dad wasn't up to the work. That he'd insist on helping us and that it might kill him."

*

It was almost midnight when Eva finally settled into a hot bath and poured herself a large glass of vodka. For a while she hesitated about calling her brother, but then the vodka took matters in hand, and Eva picked up the receiver right in the tub.

"Listen up, brother," she said without greeting him, "Malšov's off our necks. He's not going up on the roof this year. No way."

She took a swig. "Surprise, surprise. Mr. Šefl doesn't have the wood. What a coincidence. And know who made this magic happen? Guess!"

"Well?" came his expressionless voice from afar. It did not have not much interest in it.

"We're greenhorns, Iša. Two babbling bunglers. It's useless, we can't compete."

"What are you talking about, Eva?"

"What? Don't you mean who?"

She poured herself some more vodka and turned the hot water on. She had to raise her voice to drown out the noise from the faucet.

"Our omniscient mother, of course. She's got our number, don't you think?"

"Eva, can't we talk about this another time? It's midnight."

"As if I don't know what time it is! I've been on the road from stupid Malšov for ages! And know what the funniest part of it is? That Dad thinks Mother is on his side. As always. So I'm the pesky troublemaker again."

"You know, it's—"

"'You know'? What's that supposed to mean: 'you know'?"

The bathroom was full of steam. Eva waved her hands violently so she could at least see the wall.

"You know how to make a duck perform, Iša? I do. But unfortunately I learned a bit too late. It's the secret of our family. The clown on stage says: Fly, duck! And presto, the duck actually flies! Then the clown growls: Sit, duck! And bonk, at that moment the duck sits right on its bottom."

She could hear her brother yawn. It irritated her.

"The trick is that the duck simply does what it wants. The clown observes every movement it makes and a fraction of a second later gives it the appropriate command. It's not the clown making the duck perform, but the other way around!"

"So what?"

"So, our mother is the duck. Dad's the performing clown."

"Eva, I get up at four-thirty."

"The joke is that they're a blissfully happy couple. But they didn't pass their magic down to us. I've had three divorces, and your marriage is a bucket of tepid water."

"Look, do we have to discuss this tonight?"

"No! Of course not!"

The mixture of relief and annoyance at today's absurd pilgrimage flooded into Eva's blood like some weird sort of fuel.

"In our house we don't discuss anything. Night or day. In our house everyone sees only what he wants to see. For Christ's sake, don't be blind! Remember how you ran away from home?"

She knew she was heading for trouble, but it was too late to apply the brakes. What she was doing was disgraceful — one of her many disgracefully truthful deeds — but rage got the better of her.

"We didn't discuss that either, did we. Why waste words on it. So listen, brave brother of mine: you ran away in a taxi. The driver who picked you up — Mother paid him in advance. She knew you were going to run for it. She wasn't stupid enough to try to keep you home. That truck had been waiting for you for over an hour, behind the beech tree."

The water was too hot. She turned it off, but did not lower her voice.

"And that's not all, Iša. Mother set things up with the shepherd too. No, she certainly doesn't leave anything to chance! The man who took you to that hut had breakfast at our place. He roared with laughter at what an utter fool you were. 'Madam, I take my hat off to you! You're a regular fox! Madam, know what I told that idiot boy of yours? Sure, kid, I said, run off, at your age a boy can't worry about his momma!' So that's how a duck performs, see?"

There was quiet at the other end. Then Iša said calmly, "I know."

"You know what?"

"Well ... everything."

Eva's tongue suddenly felt dry in her mouth.

"Just one second: I won't fall for that. You're bluffing. How long have you known?"

"I knew it even then, that morning. You think I'd have left Mom for a month without letting her know where I was? She'd have gone crazy with worry!"

Eva sat there, motionless. The bath water was quickly growing cold. It's not true, it can't be true. If it is, I've had it wrong my entire life. Since that long-ago morning she'd despised her brother for falling for such an obvious trick, and despised her mother for stooping to it. And he'd known everything all along. Mother knew that he knew, just as brother knew what she knew, and the bond of considerate deception protected them like secret laughter. Suddenly she had an awful vision: what if that's how it had always been? What if they'd all been perfectly happy: father with mother, mother with brother, and it was only me, my eyes securely blindfolded, what if I was the only one thrust out of the circle?

"So why didn't she tell me it was all arranged?" she banged her fist on the corner of the tub. "Why did I have to go to that silly Malšov?"

"Well, you know ..." her brother shrugged from a distance, "when you're old you need to feel that you're deciding things for yourself. You want to have the impression that you can still manage. As soon as you start to feel written off, then you won't let yourself be talked into things."

It was so frightfully simple that regret and compassion caught sharply in her throat. She remembered her father waking up. He stood in the doorway like a sleepy child. Like a large, flaccid bear full of fear.

"OK, you're right," she admitted, abashed, and her tears dripped into the cooling bath. A molting bear filled with anxiety.

Yes, he was afraid they were making decisions about him while he was asleep. That his daughter would get up and fling the bitter truth in his face: that he wasn't up to Malšov anymore. That he'd never live to tear down the roof. To plaster or skim the walls. That he'd never even pick up the garbage can again.

"I'm not going to meddle anymore. I won't try to talk him into anything."

She hated herself for not having realized this on her own. For one wild second she hated virtue and truth.

"Dad's got to feel he's important."

"Yeah," her brother said, a bit taken aback, "but I wasn't talking about Dad. I was talking about Mother."

Dhum

"Don't have any illusions," the durga said maliciously. "Don't have any illusions at all!"

It was as if his final day were punishing him for daring to leave.

"What specifically do you mean?" he asked as calmly as possible.

"Like don't think you'll find me here when you get back. I'll be gone as soon as you're through that door."

"I'm not worried. Dr. Hartl will keep an eye on you."

"Hartl? The fearless phallus who was hanging around yesterday? Hey, that might be fun. He'll shake things up around here!"

Fearless phallus? Inwardly he shook his head at this expression. All durgas have caustic tongues.

"What a unique vocabulary you have. Do you have an expression for me too?" he asked, aware of the risk. Maybe it really was his final day.

She looked at him from beneath half-closed eyelids.

"You?" she said with contempt, shoving a bony finger against his breastbone. "You're a bearded fifth-grader."

The phallus was waiting for him. It sat in front of the one-way mirror as if it were a video. Nothing scandalous was happening in the waiting room — a patient was vacuuming — but Hartl was watching with an unpleasantly amused expression.

"Good peep-show."

He let it go. Hartl was not the person he would have wanted, but there was no one else to be had. His colleagues had not exactly jumped at the chance to run number seventeen (Pavilion 17, A&T: alcoholism and toxicomania, women's inpatient division) for a full three months.

"Here, I've written out the point system for you, but the nurses know it by heart. I would ask that you adhere to it strictly."

"Yeah, I've heard of it. Your system is legendary."

With a decided lack of interest, Hartl stuck the paper in his pocket.

"I can't say it's my sort of thing. I'm more into Gestalt and, I mean, imagination interests me. I won't trust old Makarenko twice."

"I'm afraid you'll have to adapt to the traditions of number seventeen," he interrupted Hartl a bit more peremptorily than he had wanted to. "I especially insist on the point system."

He was painfully aware he was wasting his breath. Hartl will shake things up, the durga had said. With the same sexually charged irresponsibility he displayed in taking on a completely unfamiliar department, Hartl would unleash a circus of spectacular chaos.

"I'm not much of a believer in speculative methods," he added in a flush of indignation toward Hartl. "Or in systemic treatment, by any means. Our work here is based on discipline." The division would fall apart before he returned.

"Oh yeah, where's the can? The men's, I mean." Here was a topic that interested Hartl. The answer was: nowhere. The department was old, converted years back in slapdash fashion, and with only one man on two whole floors there was no justification for a men's room. He shared with six nurses, one social worker, and two cleaning women. This minor detail had long since stopped bothering him.

"And it hasn't stopped you producing testosterone?" Hartl joked. "But then there's something to be said for being shut up with thirty girls. I bet your balls get a good massage."

There was a shriek out in the hallway. Probably the new one being admitted, but the nurses could handle it. He ostentatiously snapped his briefcase shut.

"So where exactly are you traveling to?" Hartl asked. "India, I know, but why? Yoga? Fantastic stuff, yoga. I did a course last summer, great for the imagination! So you aren't against my doing some yoga with the girls?"

Near his solar plexus a weak spasm of indignation was growing stronger, like a small fist squeezing shut.

"I have nothing against physical exercise; I often run sessions that have elements of yoga in them, but there's no evidence it's good for anything else."

A bearded fifth-grader, she said? A bearded fifth-grader!

There is a prevailing myth that each field is its own mirror, that a profession is a giant defense mechanism. At least the Hartls like to see it that way. Marriage counsellors are homosexuals and divorcés. For therapy, children go to the childless and to those who themselves are failed parents. The crude cloak of myth dismisses alcohol treatment as a carnival of secret lushes. It was nonsense. He had not touched alcohol for fifteen years and he had never taken drugs, even though all his colleagues had at least tried them.

His magnum opus bore the title *The Problem of Dependency and Overcoming It.* The dry, methodical sheen of his style, as well as the mountains of collated data and statistics had made it the leading work in the field.

As far as patients are concerned, Hartl was simply in error. He, on the other hand, was aware of the risks in his position. With patients he was always politely and strictly aloof. On principle he addressed them as "ladies," even those going through the wild phase of detox where, swathed in cloth, they tossed and turned on a caged bed. Never did he mix with them or the nurses. He went carefully through life, like a cat on a picket fence. He was a confirmed bachelor and the few relationships he did have — which incidentally were none that pressing — were conducted as far as possible from the clinic walls.

From time to time he would feel a strange and secret fascination for one of the ladies. It was always the same type of woman, within a noticeably narrow band of variation. She was a Durga, the ferocious mother of the gods. The goddess of violence, darkness, delirium, and depravity.

The point system, which the nurses could recite in their sleep, was the result of ten years of effort. In detailed, logical, and equitable fashion he would dole out and then take away points for the patients' trifling daily accomplishments and infractions. An example: a correct answer at evening quiz time ("List at least five benefits of abstinence!") was worth three points. An unmade bed was the same — in demerits. Every week the patients' council elected its own director, called the princess. If she did a good job of discharging her obligations, she got the largest possible reward: thirty points. Smoking outside the stated times and place (14:00-16:00, 20:00-20:30, hallway to the cloakroom) meant ten points off. Fifty points bought a day out.

The durgas, being clever to a fault, usually racked up points, took a day out, and never returned. They did not often become princess (if he could prevent it), for they felt no loyalty either to him or to the ladies. In a week they could turn the group's morale upside down. Childless and completely unmaternal, they were usually ravaged by countless abortions.

Durgas have narrow eyes, scrawny, foxlike snouts, and a curious oil-free, powdery filth. The votive abstraction of their faces reveals virgin martyrs rejoicing on their fiery beds, especially when they have secured a source of drugs. Often they are educated and very sharp, but they use their cleverness like snakes use their poison fangs. A black moon shines from their eyes. He imagined them to have a winelike flavor. Their speech could be wily and quick. Yet they were as bitterly beautiful and neglected as an October grave.

He subjected himself to a similarly demanding discipline and a decidedly stricter point system. The system came from a book fate had sent his way at sixteen, which had influenced his life forever after. It was American and was called *Yoga in a Hundred Days.* (The titles *Italian in a Hundred Days, Chess in a Hundred Days,* and a score of others had been published in the same series, a fact he was of course unaware of.) The book laid out its exercise program with American thoroughness and an exalted faith in systems. Each activity was scored according to its difficulty. Bonus points were awarded for additional holding time.

It was then he began keeping daily score of the points he achieved. He had been doing it for nineteen years now, non-stop. Later he added positions the book did not contain, and plotted their points using coordinates: x-axis for the number of minutes practiced, y-axis for difficulty. He had a notepad where he would write his totals out each evening. It was the most intimate part of his existence, at least in the material world. He never showed it to anyone. He never spoke of it to anyone.

At sixteen he longed to go to India. At seventeen he promised himself firmly that one day he would.

Actually, his first inspiration was not yoga, but pure, bone-chilling Buddhism. To escape the snares of cause and effect, to evaporate into the pure void. Nothing less than the absolute itself was worthy of acceptance.

He shocked his parents, both tepid Christians, when he stopped eating meat (fleeing his mother's cooking and her fat, smothering love) and shaved his head bare. It was small and round like a beggar's bowl. He decided to live as a Buddhist monk.

All he achieved was to suddenly look thirteen again. There was a constant draft on his bare head. He felt his brain was freezing over. Twice that winter they pricked his eardrums. It didn't even help his spirituality.

He let his hair grow back and never shaved off his beard, which had just started to sprout, somewhat late. But he did trim it into a tidy goatee. Meat was still out of the question, to the great regret of his mother, for whom cooking was an abundant, meaty source of joy.

Even today he can visualize his shivering bare head, and the memory of it causes him especial disappointment. His sacrifice did not help him attain Nirvana. He abandoned Buddhism and chose the way of yoga, that flowered path full of symbols. Ever since, he has preferred to keep his head warm, and from October onward will not go out bareheaded. He wears hats.

On that shining path, full of Lotuses and Lights, mythical beasts, nymphs, and miracle-workers, the Durga represents the frightening aspect of motherhood. She renounces and devours her children, despises the world of phenomena, and catapults out of reality like a pilot out of a burning plane. She is mischievous, capricious, and duplicitous by turns, and never lets herself be hoodwinked. Blood, raw meat, intoxicating drinks, and goats are sacrificed to her. She can be appeased by ritual suicide. Her laughter shakes the bones of the dead; no one can hear it without losing all certitude. A long, black tongue hangs from her mouth. Sparks of nothingness illuminate her in the darkness. Her mantra is *dhum*.

The time and country in which his plan took shape were not at all conducive to its success. He gave over half his life to it. It demanded sacrifices — like every properly accredited spiritual goal, incidentally. The energy he expended overcoming the obstacles in his path would have powered a small factory. He has sacrificed his vacation from last year, this year, and part of next year as well. He has sacrificed practically all his savings.

At thirty-five, he has succeeded. He has an exit visa, a plane ticket, and an invitation to a "Yoga Centre" somewhere in the south of India. Even a replacement — the weakest point in his program, which had threatened to wreck the entire plan — has now been secured: Hartl. His spartan rucksack is packed, with a precious five hundred U.S. dollars sewn into an inner pocket. Tomorrow is the day he departs.

His mother is small and is constantly laughing. She finishes her sentences with laughter even when there is nothing laughable about them. Wiping her teary eyes with the back of her hand, she says apologetically, "Why do I find everything so funny!"

He inherited his small stature from her, and a vigilantly guarded tendency toward plumpness, which has no chance against the hundreds of points he racks up daily. He inherited neither the lively briskness of chubby sprites nor their laughter.

His father was absent, so to speak. The man had spent most of his time in his room. Although he owned a hearing aid, he usually carried it in his pocket. He never heard when they knocked on his door. Not long ago he had died, leaving no visible trace. If he had inherited anything from his father, he did not know what it was.

"How about a baby, sonny?" his mother would ask regularly, breaking into loud laughter immediately afterward. "I know you're a terribly busy man, no time to get married, but don't worry, I'll bring him up for you!" She seemed blissfully oblivious to any role the prospective other parent might play. "Don't forget to come back from that Shangri-La of yours. And don't pull your long faces at people there, they won't like it!"

She would often rub the bridge of his nose with her thumb, right where his wrinkles met, "so you won't be such a sourpuss." The place would itch long after.

"Watch out you don't overeat, Mom. You know what I told you about those varicose veins!"

"Oh please! What do I have left in the world besides those few miserable goodies?" she would say, exploding in mournful laughter. The problem of dependency and overcoming it.

A durga in ward seventeen means failure. Mostly they constitute that unfortunate percent or two in the column labeled *Treatment Interrupted.* They escape from the wards and often take drugs during their therapy. Their eyes shine too brightly in their scrawny, foxlike snouts.

This last one had even studied medicine before pervitin, a homemade amphetamine known in underworld slang as "nerve whip," put an end to that. Her three years of study had left her with some jargon and a skepticism of psychiatry bordering on hatred.

"I'll tell you what you are: voyeurs with prescription glasses. And still you don't see fuck-all, 'cause you're totally out of it! You take away the one thing we have and give us absolutely nothing in return."

"Don't forget that sometimes in doing so we save your life."

"Know where you can put that sorta life?"

A banal conversation he had had a hundred times. Only

now a bony regret grabbed at him, probably an inevitable mark of his final day.

"I don't expect us to share the same scale of values; otherwise we wouldn't be sitting here together."

What he wanted to say was: we'd be sitting together somewhere else, but he knew it wasn't true. With durgas it was here or nowhere. *Dhum!*

"But I took the Hippocratic oath and that requires me to save your life first, and only later ask what sense there is in it."

Unselfconsciously she peeled a layer of skin from her chapped lips, examined it carefully, and then began to pulverize it between teeth that had not seen a dentist in ages.

"You ever try it?" she said.

"I assume you mean drugs. I drank wine when I was a student, and other than that just black coffee."

"Lucky you!" was her provocative retort. "Only someone completely out of touch would do a crappy job like this."

One durga, whom he thought he had parted with on good terms (she hadn't run away but had discontinued treatment for a kidney operation) had sent him a letter. Over the address it said: *Sadist Fascist Onanist* and the text ran: "You don't know shit about BLISS!!!"

He wanted to believe she'd written it under the influence of a volatile combination of hashish and beer, even though as a doctor he should not have wanted that. No, he expected no satisfaction from his work. He had been soberly aware of that when he began.

He was already at the door, with one foot in southern India, and she was about to make her escape, and yet she added:

"You still think you can change us. We all make fun of you.

Your whole life is a mistake. No one changes, not ever, even if they stand on their head."

Two durgas were already dead. They had found one of them about a month ago in the boiler room of ward seventeen. She had a plastic shopping bag over her head, still reeking from alcohol and tied firmly beneath her chin with panty hose.

*

"Well, you're the logical one," Hartl announced. There was an implicit sneer in it: you're just one of those reductionist western types.

Yes, but beneath that was a deeper layer and, as he firmly believed, a more authentic one. An austere, insistent yearning for the Holy Spirit, which had taken the form of Indian spirituality, coupled with the awareness that this was only one of its many veils.

He spent hours in his meditation bubble. There would be a firm silence around him, a pair of parentheses in the midst of a passionate sentence, a membrane rigid as a fetal sac. His striving was deep and genuine, confirmed day after day. Sometimes, rarely, he had the feeling he was close to his goal. But he knew that he was not yet ripe, because he still lacked a Teacher.

"When the pupil is ready, the guru comes," that American book had told him, at the age when such striking slogans comfort us. He believed it. It was an anchor of hope, lodged in the deepest sea-bed of the End. But how many more points? What did it mean to be ready?

He did not hurry. He was exceedingly patient. (Hartl: "Fantastic stuff, yoga. I did a course last summer!") If need be, he would wait till he dropped. His belief in the karmic logic of crime and punishment, merit and reward, was unflagging. It was what he found most captivating about yoga: the colossal point system of karma. The clear, inexorable equity of a Spirit incapable of judicial error.

The deepest dream beneath the lid of his daily reverie: he enters a room lit so sparsely that the dream is not set against any specific background. In the middle of the room sits the Teacher. From the first moment it is obvious. They recognize each other, confidently, completely. "How long I have waited for you!" both say in their wordless tongue. There is nothing left but to bow.

Of course, his ladies were inclined to tout their trips there and back as enticingly as they could: gushes of never-seen colors and incandescent spits turning between ecstasy and torture. He did not enjoy hearing about them, especially in public conversations; it retarded the healing process, he claimed. The truth was that it disturbed him. He neither needed nor wanted this sort of psychedelicizing. His pillar of firmament was narrow and bare. A rigid bubble of silence, the eye of the hurricane — this is what he wanted.

True, sometimes it even happened to him — very fleetingly and rarely — that the flares of consciousness inside him were garbed in blissful colors, an irrepressible rapture surged two or three decimeters up his spine, the eye of the hurricane threatened to yield to a whirlwind and tear his membrane apart. The membrane pulsated and grew hot, swelling like a blood-filled sac; IT was almost close enough to touch. One barely perceptible movement, and IT WOULD HAPPEN.

The membrane always remained intact. At the last moment anxiety would course through him, and the condition would dissipate as quickly as it arose, leaving him on the bare plain of his own emptiness.

Recently the first signs of aging had begun to trouble him: an as of yet insignificant delay when urinating and unpleasant nighttime awakenings with burning pins and needles. It was time, high time to depart, to go where — as it said, word for word, in the invitation letter — they were all awaiting him with love.

The night before his departure he slept rather uneasily. Before awakening he had a dream: he is on his way, but at the last minute remembers that he has left his hat at home. He returns, hastily opens his wardrobe, and finds his father sitting in it, naked. He closes the wardrobe just as hastily, pretending not to have noticed anything. I will have to make do without my hat, is the last thought he wakes with, as he runs in his dream out onto the sidewalk.

The plane trip still had European features. The stewardesses, although dressed in saris, spoke perfect English. The tiny drink bottles, practically unspillable, were strange, but in a Western way. From the moment he stepped onto the hot Indian soil, though, he found himself in another world. The last word he could read was the EXIT at the airport gate.

A train bore him through the night like a time machine, carrying him back into childhood illiteracy. All the schools he had passed through, his doctorate, two higher qualifications, all for naught. He did not understand a word; the station signs said nothing to him.

In the middle of the night, in a light half-sleep, he heard a piercing cry. The compartment emptied out, a host of people trundled down the corridor, and the train stopped in the thick, exotic darkness. He had no idea what had happened. An accident? A crime? Was his life in danger? He sat, forgotten, in the empty compartment, his heart thudding in his head, and large mosquitoes, whining ampules of his blood, criss-crossed the stifling space.

Suddenly the train started again and the compartment filled. He never found out what had happened. This day was the first in more than fifteen years that he could not give himself even a single point.

(Fifteen years before, in a rebellious "dark night of the soul," he had drunk himself practically into oblivion. He had been rejected quite roughly by a girl, a weak shadow of a durga in the still childish face of an exemplary student. He felt so awful he could have died. From that moment on he never drank and had never been rejected.)

The letter he had received from India bore the signature of the center's director, his guru. The signature was large, labored, and full of decorative strokes; it betrayed a lack of familiarity with western penmanship. Underneath it was a stamp: *Swami Devananda Paramahamsa, Chief of Yoga Centre.* Paramahamsa means “Highest Soul” and it is an honorific title, a registered trademark for complete enlightenment.

With the letter came a flier containing a short biography of the swami. He was sixty-nine and since twenty-two had performed “multiples miracles.” At the top was his likeness, but the colors had run astrally together, so that the swami’s face, just as in his dream, was merely a cipher, fertile in its mysteriousness.

After more than thirty hours’ travel, he finally arrived in the full sun of midday. Thirsty, dirty, the t-shirt he had put on that morning at the train station already dripping with sweat, but there, at last.

A taxi took him around the city’s perimeter and rode for a long while down dusty roads. Then it stopped, the driver pointed majestically — we are here! — and the pilgrim was standing on the threshold of the ashram.

He was too tired to feel surprise. Just a certain dull wonder that the ashram looked like a modern apartment building in Prague. Four floors, a bare rectangle, peeling paint. Two elevators, one out of order. Everywhere English signs and arrows: *Meditation Hall, Club, Rooms.*

At the reception office a bespectacled Indian woman took his passport. She looked him over and picked up the telephone. As she spoke into the receiver in breakneck Hindi, she began to gesture for him to leave the room. Confused, he obeyed, made his exit, and found himself in a corridor.

A tiny, lively Indian man came running down the dark hallway crosshatched with sunlight from the narrow windows.

As he trotted past the sharp bands of light, he seemed like a runner leaping hurdles. He could have been twenty-five, thirty at the most. He wore a saffron robe and a green knit ski-hat.

"My name is Swami Garudananda," he said to the visitor in English, his eyes suggestive of a clever monkey. He had a strong Indian accent, but put out his hand like a European. "At the moment, I run the Yoga Centre for Swami Devananda, who travels and will be gone for half a year. I am infinitely happy that you are here. How long I expect you!"

There are times when fate turns gradually around on its axis to show us a different projection against the backdrop, another shadow of the same shape. Now was such a time.

He was still too worn out to notice the bitter freshness of disappointment. In the way that a fabric's bright colors fade over time, he slowly realized that his guru was not there. He had come in the off-season. He had jeopardized a department fifteen years in the making with a risky replacement of dubious quality, so he could put his closely guarded spirituality into the hands of this little boy, some sort of vice-guru, this square root of his secret hopes. With that fascinating inexactitude that marks the fulfillment of prophecies and yearnings, he had reached the threshold of his goal: the initial sentence had been uttered.

"A problem is developed," the Indian continued as he scurried through the building. "A compatriot of yours — a Serb woman — causes a certain problem. Unfortunately she speaks only Serbian. You surely will understand her."

He let the factual mistake pass, for he did not want his first contact with his Teacher — even such a spurious one as this — to be a correction or qualification. Calling the Czech lands part of Serbia (or vice versa) was a mistake commonly made even by foreigners considerably closer to both countries.

"She reveres our guru, Swami Devananda, and has fallen into a state of trance. Undoubtedly she struck a rapport with him. Of course she does not take nourishment."

"Is she drinking?" he asked mechanically, as he would have done at the clinic.

"No."

"How long has it been?"

"It is the fourth day, as far as we know. She does not eat, drink, or sleep. She is broken all contact with the outside world. She is in rapport only with the Swami-ji. In all probability she now approaches the state of liberation."

He smiled at his guest with the sincere smile of a wily boy, like those who had run alongside the train, hands outstretched, and kept smiling even when they were given nothing.

"And how can I help you?"

"We would be grateful if you would examine her. If you would tell us, as a doctor, to what extent her health is at risk," the Indian answered cautiously. So he knew. That four days without taking liquids, especially in this oppressive heat, could start an irreversible process. The Serb was most probably a wild psychotic. He could not count on psychopharmaceuticals being available here.

"We will await your opinion before deciding," Garudananda said. "You are a psychiatrist, after all, true?"

The door at the end of the hallway opened. A psychiatrist — that he was.

⁂

He found himself in a darkened chamber filled with furniture he could as of yet only sense. His sight slowly adjusted to the darkness. Then, in the corner of the room, he spotted a bulky female form on rumpled blankets.

He approached her with the natural shyness of a newcomer, but he immediately realized she was not aware of him at all. She was sitting bent forward, her corpulent back limp and rounded, slowly swaying. Between their swollen lids, her eyes stared fixedly at the wall, pinned to which was a picture of Devananda in a wreath of wilting flowers. It was probably the same one as on the flyer, but a technologically better reproduction. The Serb had fastened the unmoving pupils of her eyes on him, mumbling monotonously without rest.

He was aware that they were expecting something from him. Three steps behind him stood the small swami and another man in an orange robe, who had appeared out of nowhere.

"Hello!" he said softly in Czech, although he knew full well that the woman was not tuned in. Both men probably thought he had said something in Serbian. It made absolutely no difference. He had seen people in this state before and even a hammer blow wouldn't have brought the Serb out of it.

"Ma'am," he continued in Czech, "I'm a doctor and I want to help you."

He felt like a charlatan, but he had no idea what else to do. He took the woman's wrist and checked her pulse. This merely transferred his deception from word to deed, because at this point what could her pulse possibly tell him?

The Serb was not a durga, quite the opposite. She was a fat, ordinary woman with home-dyed hair, whose gray roots gave the impression that she was close to sixty and had been here over two months. She was the sort who in villages gets called "auntie" or, somewhat disparagingly, "mother." Only that deliriously happy expression lifted her above the most everyday everydayness.

The hand he had been holding for too long seemed not to belong to the rest of the Serb woman's body, nor to her soul. When he carefully let it go, it slipped back gently along her side and then rose ethereally, as if it were weightless, landing back on her lap.

"Has anyone tried giving her fluids?" he said aloud.

"They were offered to her, of course, but as you can see, she doesn't show the least interest," the second man responded in noticeably cleaner English. In fact, a glass of water was standing in front of the Serb. Suddenly he felt a sharp thirst. His last drink had been that morning at the train station: the dregs of tea in his thermos.

"Is there another doctor around, for a consultation?" he asked, playing for time.

"There's an Australian, a veterinarian, but he's away from the ashram at the moment."

A veterinarian? Might as well be back in Australia.

"There is one nurse here, if you need help. What's your opinion of the situation?"

Four days, he thought to himself. The immediate risk is small, but in two or three days it could be too late, and then her exit was almost certain.

"I'll decide this evening," he said in the tone he used with the nurses in Prague.

*

They led him into the room he was to share for the next quarter of a year with the absent veterinarian. He fell onto the hard, narrow cot like a stone into a lake, and in five seconds he was asleep.

He woke at dusk, irritated, with the feeling that someone through the wall had thoughtlessly turned up the radio. Waves of wailing voices rose, broke against a gong stroke, and then with the same wails descended. Evening prayers, he realized. I must have overslept, I'm not where I ought to be.

A respectful cough came from the gloom, almost like in a play. The man who had visited the Serb with him (the realization slowly surfaced in his warm, befogged mind) was sitting on the floor at the foot of his bed.

"Are you awake, doctor? I've been waiting here for you. I thought I'd explain to you what's going on." He spoke fluently and his pronunciation was clear. "Let me introduce myself. My name here is Kumar. I'm from Britain, but this is my ninth year in the ashram and I'm never going back to Europe."

He sat up in bed, somewhat ashamed of his condition. At home he bathed twice a day: mornings at the clinic, evenings after exercising at home. The man gave him a slight smile.

"Just so you know, you're in a rather awkward situation. This case has provoked sharp debate right from the start. Whichever way you decide, you'll meet opposition from one side or another. It's quite a delicate matter, you see."

Still tangled in the spider's web of sleep, he felt his heavy, sour tongue sticking to his palate. He did not want to decide or discuss anything. He wanted to take a bath, brush his teeth, and roll back up in the blankets. Instead he stood up, so at least he could comb his hair.

"There are some very orthodox old Indians here, although it's not a matter of age or race. One extreme faction simply believes that this lady has spiritually overtaken all of us. No one has the right to meddle in processes of this sort. If she dies in the next few days, it will be the highest blessing. She will free herself from the torment of cause and effect. Of course ... of course ..." — the Briton made a dance-like, roundabout gesture with his finger — "... in the eyes of your government we are responsible for her life, isn't that so?"

The same mistake again, but he couldn't face correcting anyone.

"You can see our predicament."

"Yes ... and what do you think about it?"

A shrug. "Me? I'm just letting you know the score. Our swami-ji has put his complete trust in you, and whatever you decide will be accepted without question. But be prepared for the fact that there will be disagreement, possibly hostility. There are many, many ..." — once again that gesture as he searched for the exact word — "... many different forces in this ashram."

The rising and falling of the evening prayer behind the wall continued unchanged.

"Swami Garudananda," the Briton said in a hushed, fervent tone, "is one of the greatest spiritual beings of our age, if not the very greatest. But his time is yet to come."

There was a sudden imperative in his eyes, as if he were expecting assent. What was there to say?

"I'd like to see the lady again."

Kumar stood up, nodded, and added with British courtesy:

"I'm quite sure you'll take the right decision. If you don't mind, I'll accompany you."

He was aware of being watched. A small group paused in their conversation as the two of them passed, and somewhere a door opened a crack and then closed again. It was only now he realized that he didn't know the number of his own room. How would he find it in that anonymous corridor? But he put it out of his head. Later.

The Serb was sitting on her blanket; nothing had moved, although a table lamp had been lit in a corner. The singing, now somewhat dampened by distance, spun round in a circle like the cycle of seasons.

The Briton discreetly vanished. For the first time, he was alone with the woman. She had the same expression of all-engulfing bliss in her eyes, which glittered like lifeless fish. Occasionally she would twitch, like a patient under light anesthesia. Her quiet muttering seemed to escape rather than issue from her mouth. It could have been fragments of Serbian or just a stream of random sounds her mind had already stopped monitoring. Or the "gift of the Holy Spirit," fiery tongues raining down on the apostles' heads. This was the question, and he was to fill in the answer.

He sat on the floor next to the Serb. For a moment he fancied that she was aware of his presence. She watched him slyly from beneath half-closed lids. She had that same intense yet absent glance often seen in self-portraits.

In the dark outside, an invisible bird shrieked and fell silent. A rivulet of sweat trickled down the woman's face. Her body gave off a vigorous, carnal odor.

She should lose at least twenty-five pounds; this thought suddenly came to him from somewhere off in a corner of his brain. It's a terrible strain on the coronary system. His glance slid to her legs — did she have varicose veins? — but the legs were not visible beneath the swathe of material. A few days of fasting would only do her good.

There was a time, one particular time not too long ago in Prague, when he was at the bank, signing a check, conscious of the fact that he was drawing his savings down to nothing. A sneaking thought said to him: Why not? I'm never coming back, anyway.

He had honorably waited out the whole false period of his youth, now slowly but surely drawing to a close. He had lived without question, with the discipline of a parachutist, crouched over, calf muscles tense, waiting for permission to jump. Somewhere in the depths of his dreams he longed to shed his European lab coat with no regrets and become his true self: but even he did not know what he meant by this, and it is the way of such things that he would not know until he had crossed that threshold.

The glass of water was still standing in front of the Serb, as it had been earlier that day; half-dead mosquitoes now floated on its surface. Who has the right to snip the golden thread of her blessedness? And if there were no golden thread, if the path were a false one, if there were no Lotuses or Lights, white gurus or karma, if — alas! — there were no escape from the suffering of this world, then who truly had the right to deprive her of such a happy death?

But if he let her die without help, now, here, before his very eyes, he would have nowhere to go back to. Then, in all honesty, he would have to set aside his medical diploma, and his faith in the Lotuses and Lights would have to surpass all reasonable bounds.

A sudden, unaccustomed rage surged through him. He was furious at that phony guru, that assistant master, that lying little monkey substitute. That's who was responsible! He had no right to treacherously fob it off on someone else, on a defenseless novice! And Swami Devananda? Why wasn't he here? Couldn't he hear how urgently he was being called? Where had he put his holy hearing aid? Why didn't he perform another of his "multiples miracles"?

Beneath his wrath lay an anxiety far more severe: what if it were all a test? A magnificent tableau for an initiation ceremony. It was an experiment with one black ball and one white one — he would either win, or lose.

He was oppressed by the feeling that someone was pacing impatiently outside the door. When he had awakened today to find Kumar peering into his face, he had lost his sense of security. Perhaps they were watching his every step. The one-way mirror of clairvoyance allowed the gurus to observe him, even through closed doors. The building held its breath and waited — a building, as Kumar had said, full of different forces.

He turned to face the Serb again. As the room darkened, her eyes opened. The woman licked her chapped lips slowly and languidly.

"What should I do?" he asked her suddenly, impulsively. "What would you like me to do?"

She mumbled something, still running her dry tongue along her dry lips.

"I don't want to hurt you. Please believe me. I only want what's right for you."

No one, not even his patients, had ever depended on him so terribly, so completely. If his faith were correct, if there were Lotuses and Lights, this relationship would cross even the boundary of death. He would be engaged, karmically Forever, to this woman, whose existence he had been unaware of before this morning.

He breathed deeply and then said out loud, fully conscious of his words: "Oh God! Help me!"

The Serb fastened her empty eyes on him. Had she seen him? Maybe yes, maybe no. In her mumbling there was a short cascade of sounds that rolled like a small wave of laughter: but it might have been his imagination. Emptiness filled the hollow just behind his breastbone. Suddenly he made his decision.

He averted his eyes from the woman and strode quickly across the room. He threw open the door. To his surprise there was no one behind it. The long, deserted hallway stretched out before him in the flickering light. He realized that he could no longer hear the prayers.

*

"I want to speak with Swami Garudananda," he said to an Indian receptionist in jeans.

"I cannot call him now; he is in meditation."

"It's urgent."

"I am sorry, but it is not possible to disturb the swami."

"It's a matter of life and death for your communicant."

The Indian had already said all she intended to. He saw no

reason to restrain himself. The wrinkles above his nose deepened and he slammed his fist down on the table:

"I am a doctor, I am responsible for her. I'm warning you! Her vital functions could break down. Delay is a crime on both humanitarian and legal grounds!"

The Indian gave a slight shrug.

Garudananda did in fact come, about two hours later. When he heard the verdict (the woman must be treated without delay and her body's fluids rapidly replenished), his shrewd, dark eyes betrayed a certain relief.

It turned out that this spiritual hotel had a surprisingly serviceable clinic. Someone sent for three of the "novices." Two men showed up, and one Canadian woman, middle-aged and dressed in a sari: forlorn, skinny, with all the glamour of a swamp flower, the unmistakable mark of the durga on her forehead.

There were no introductions; they immediately fell into working mode. He gave practical instructions, leaving the physical side to them. Almost indifferently, he watched as they capably lifted the Serb under her arms and beneath her knees, and strapped her to a bed. She offered surprisingly little resisance, as if she were not even present in that fat, sweaty body. There was merely a brief increase in her mumbling as they carried her through the door.

From there on in it was a matter of routine. The Canadian was, as it turned out, a competent nurse, and under his supervision she put a drip into the Serb's forearm. The Serb did not even flinch as the needle slipped smoothly into her vein.

He suddenly wondered which faction these three belonged to. Were they judging him? Did they approve of his decision? Were they future friends or enemies in this night-enfolded house, where he had arrived less than a day ago and still had three months to spend?

The mumbling gradually grew weaker. Soon the body slackened, and the glistening whites of her eyes disappeared behind their swollen lids. From the outside it seemed the Serb was sleeping peacefully.

He sent his assistants away, telling them he would monitor the woman himself. They nodded and impassively said good-bye. There was no commentary on what had transpired. He sat down by the Serb's bed and suddenly felt the whole weight of his journey. He realized vaguely that he would have to stay here tonight, since he would not be able to find his room.

The Canadian suddenly turned around in the doorway. She was the last of the three to leave, and for the first time she looked him straight in the eyes. There was such contempt in her thin, foxlike face that his fingertips went cold. Of course, he could have been wrong; the contact was too brief, and durgas always look contemptuous. Still, in that moment he lost his last shred of hope.

The durga closed the door behind her; the Serb slept on. It was quiet in the building. He must have briefly fallen asleep in the chair, because suddenly he opened a drawer and his watch was lying in it.

He had received the watch from his mother as a Christmas present when he was eight. Soon thereafter he was at a children's carnival and a magician did a trick that charmed it off his wrist. Before the boy's very eyes, in full sight of everyone in the hall, the man threw it into a mortar bigger than a bucket and ground it to a powder. For a few horrible minutes he thought he would never be able to go home. Then the magician twirled a handkerchief over the mortar and pulled out the watch, whole and unharmed. The boy was relieved that at least he could go home now, but he did not put the watch back on, and he no longer wanted to wear it. He had lost his trust in it: he could not be sure that it was in fact the same one, and at night he would shut it up in the bottom of his drawer.

He woke to find his leg had fallen asleep. It prickled unpleasantly. He stood up to stretch a bit, and realized it was almost one in the morning. Yesterday was the third time, since the day he had needlessly shaved his head, that he had failed to get even a single point.

O durga, mother of disillusion,
drinking blood, devouring raw meat,
mother of all gods and goddesses,
ruler of the earth,
staring blankly, dancing without rest,
fearsome in your greatness,
honor be to you,
dhum!

The Thirty-Sixth Chicken of Master Wu

à V. L.

"Your nephew is here, Master," the serving boy announced in a funereal voice, supposing that it made him sound educated. "He would gladly undergo a hundred more incarnations for the privilege of greeting you."

Wu knitted his eyebrows until their spiky white hairs converged beneath his forehead. He had no taste for yet another commentary on the combination of *sin* and *sa* syllables, but did not see how he could avoid it. The aroma Wu himself had named "porcelain maiden" was surely wafting along the corridors all the way to the court; in all the empire no one else had the skill to prepare the porcelain maiden. Only Wu. Only he! He and only he!

He felt a wearisome pressure in his head, the hollow pressure of several indistinct ideas ("fame — nakedness — nowhere to hide"), but there was no time to consider them: he had just lit the flames, and with painstaking care he was swinging the pan in an arc three thumbs wide and three-quarters-of-a-thumb high. Only thus could the "maiden" truly be released.

"Let him enter."

A tubby, aging youth was standing in the doorway, shifting from foot to foot. He shuffled awkwardly along the wall into the room. His belly was soft and he teetered on long, thin legs like a wading bird.

"It's hot," the youth said reproachfully.

"Lots hot," he added after a moment.

He took off his hat and mopped his balding head and his short, chafed neck with a none-too-clean handkerchief. The odor of his sweat intermingled with the porcelain maiden, and only Wu's six-year monastic education in controlling his inner demons allowed him to hide his distaste. He was nearly certain no one would notice that aberrant moment in the final product, but nonetheless all hope of perfection was irrevocably gone. At the most critical juncture, when the pieces of meat first mystially united with the blue-burning sauce of Jena beans and pepper, an alien stench had permeated them — and that never helped matters. Still, Wu said to himself, those two geese — meaning the empress and her oldest daughter — they won't notice it, but as for me, I would never let it touch my tongue.

"Thank you, exalted one, for–stooping–to–my–humble–insignificance," he mumbled. It took far less time to say than it does to read. Centuries of misuse and age-old affectation had ground this common idiom down to a few muddled, utterly meaningless syllables. The poet looked at the round chair as if wondering what to do with it, and then sat heavily down.

"Whatcha cooking?" he said without interest.

What a question! It stung Wu, but lightly, like a flea. Everyone knew the porcelain maiden. Even his nephew had eaten at least his weight's worth; he should know that aroma by now! What if I asked him: so you write poems, is that it? Never heard of them. No one recites them! — His inner demons toyed briefly with the idea of saying this out loud, but Wu did not have the time just now.

"Dinner for the empress," he answered calmly.

The meal was now almost ready. All that remained was to pour it into stone bowls rubbed generously with a bitter root. Wu did not usually rub the bowls himself, but yesterday he had caught a plump little girl peeling the root with fingernails that were horrendously dirty. He was so infuriated that he whacked her with a large ladle. She whimpered for a while and this morning made herself scarce — well, she was evidently afraid, probably off complaining to some hysterical aunt of hers that she couldn't take that old madman anymore.

Alone! All on my own! the demons wailed, and from the height of a child's arm Wu began precisely and ever so carefully to pour the pungent substance into the steaming bowls. When the moist maiden touched the sizzling stoneware it underwent a final, triumphant tremble. The vitreous meat writhed and congealed, as if it wanted to flocculate, but it held fast, its surface splitting slightly open. It now looked like the frozen skin of a very pale girl, with a polished tinge akin to that of old miniatures. Wu knew this was the only way to achieve a gradation of flavors. In the meat's tiny cracks, the juices had not uniformly hardened, and the crust had become a concentrate of the concoction's spicy apex: a plume of taste, its coloratura.

Wu, as always at that moment, remembered the day he had discovered the trick with the hot bowl. He was not quite thirty and had run non-stop out toward the Buried Wells, nearly delirious with a high, ringing joy.

"The empressetta eats too much," the poet said indifferently, undoing his belt to let his belly flop out. "The princessina too. They're glutton-guts."

It was the poet's habit to mutilate the most common of words, as if he didn't even know his own language. And to think his teacher had been one of the empire's most famous grammarians! At fifteen Wu's nephew had put out his instructor's eye in a scuffle and was immediately exiled to the provinces. Only his family connection to Wu and, at the time, Wu's strong hand, had enabled him to return years later.

The poet stuck his hand under the silk.

"Have you spoken with the censor?" he asked, yawning. From the wild rippling of the ribbons he appeared to be scratching his belly most energetically.

Ah, so that's why you're poking around here! Wu thought, irritated. You've come to find out whether this year they'll finally have a public reading of your ... your ... He hesitated, but the only thing that came to mind were some words mutilated in his nephew's style, so he stopped trying to pin down the concept. Well, you can wait, boy, you can wait. I think I already do more for you than I should by letting you parasitize the family name — and heaven knows it's never done anything for me. But for me to dishonor it further by advancing your ... your ... It was the same problem as before, and Wu abandoned his ruminations.

"The censors," he said severely, "are drowning in work just now. Over a hundred poems came in for the emperor's birthday celebration contest. The censors have locked themselves in the library and have been studying them for days."

His nephew stared sleepily at the smoke-stained ceiling as if this answer had nothing to do with him. The porcelain maiden became more delicate by the moment; it evaporated into oblivion like a dream before waking, and what was left behind was a taste just as evanescent, haunting and hollow. His nephew could probably no longer smell it, Wu realized, and soon, after twice the time, it would desert Wu as well. How many times have I lost her already, and where does she disappear to? I'll never know.

"The emperor will probably disappear," his nephew said suddenly, in the expressionless tone he always used. "I figured it out by doing a structural analysis of the last hundred years of court poetry."

Here there should be a brief aside. It concerns the translator's responsibility for the words *structural analysis*, for the words *censor, parasitize, coloratura* and, in the end, for the majority of others.

There are two basic ways to translate what has not yet come to be and what no longer is. One is with the eternal present's abbreviated arc, in the belief that the sense of words and things endures and, like Zeno's arrow, hangs in flight. The other keeps to Babel's model, clinging anxiously to the literal meaning of individual words confined to the solitary cell of their place and time. We choose the first method, but this does not mean it is the better one. Wu's nephew definitely did not say *structural analysis,* but if we were to take this to extremes, then he was not a *nephew,* but a *second left blood with male sound,* because that is how the language in question characterizes this relationship.

The word *censor,* in its professional sense, is roughly the same as we picture it today. *Head censor* — so we know in advance what is meant — is not a profession, but a title, a pedestal of honor and imperial might, and, it must be said, quite a high pedestal indeed.

"What did you say?" Wu sputtered. He was not asking about the emperor's fate; he refused so thoroughly to take this seriously that he forgot it at once. "Where did you happen on the last hundred years of court poems?"

"I have them." The poet shrugged.

"Where did you get them from?" Wu pressed him.

"From the bibliotheca. It's not like anyone reads them; the dust on them was a finger deep. I simply took them."

Wu raised his eyes to the heavens. The poet suddenly became wary. He glanced around and then leaned over.

"I figured it out!" he whispered in a theatrical whisper. "If only it's not too late! Sit down, let me explain."

Wu did not sit down. He was an old man and deeply disliked getting up again afterward. At this hour, when the servants had taken the dishes away and swept out the drifts of ash, the kitchen was quiet for the first time all day. Tense, vigilant, Wu devoted his nights to experimentation. He slept little, and many a time it was only when the stars had left their fatal conjunctions and the great crimson parrots had begun to squawk over the eastern gates, that he finally put aside his bowls and ingredients and plunged his worn, slender tongue into water.

"They've compared him to an elephant eight hundred twenty-two times already!" the poet announced with a passionate fervor Wu had not seen before — at least not since the time when, as a boy, he had shouted at Wu that he'd been in the right in that argument with his teacher and a poke in the eye couldn't alter this basic fact. Except then he'd been fifteen.

"I'm sure as sure can be! I've checked it over countless times! No one must ever do it again, ever! It's ... it's death!"

Wu stared in surprise at his nephew's pockmarked skin: agitation had made a childhood scar reemerge like a long-gone, wind-blasted epitaph on a gravestone.

"Why shouldn't they?" he said evenly. "I'm not an expert on poetry, but as a simile it seems to me both accurate and respectful."

The poet clenched his fists.

"The devil take accuracy! To hell with respectfulness! They've gone too far! And soon there will be retribution!"

Wu had no idea what his nephew meant. His allegations seemed likely, even though it would never have occurred to Wu to count. Comparing the emperor to an elephant was so common that no one gave it a second thought. The elephant's suitability derived from its beauty as well as from its strength, not to mention the esteem it had enjoyed in the empire since time immemorial. The commemorative poems all the empire's poets entered in the emperor's yearly birthday contest positively teemed with elephants, every time. But Wu still could not conceive what anyone could have against this. It had always been thus, ever since he could remember, under the emperor's father, grandfather, and probably even beyond, until the past's thread was broken by war or earthquake.

"Poets don't create anymore!" his nephew hissed. "They just steal from each other! They're worse than grave robbers. They're hyenas!"

"Careful, boy! Take care!" Wu raised his voice. "No celebratory poem was ever stolen! The emperor's censors are ever so strict on that point! The punishment for stealing a contest poem is worse nowadays than for trespassing!"

His nephew, seated, stomped his feet on the floor.

"Last year Mr. Hayo won with the poem: 'The emperor's might is like the elephant leading his herd'! Does he think we've forgotten that twenty-eight years ago Asum's verse ran: 'The emperor's might bursts forth like a raging elephant'?"

"There's no comparison!" Wu adamantly insisted. His profession had given him a fine sense for the subtleties of variation. "An elephant on his own behaves completely differently from one leading a herd. Everyone knows that!"

His nephew's pale eyes grew ever so slightly paler.

"It's a conspiracy!" he whispered. "Betrayal by intellectuals. They want to destroy the emperor!"

There had been times, entire decades, when the force of these words would have swept the kitchen clean, but just now the empire lounged in a sort of political siesta. There had been no war for almost twenty years. This was mostly because the emperor was an old man (Wu, by the way, was exactly one day younger), and the most faithful of his men had kept their posts and grown old along with him. The law of the jungle and hungry battles to the death now raged further down, among the younger clerks, who were still freshly predacious and thankfully far from power. But here, at the top, where a few fading elders quivered like silken flags, the scales of danger and guilt expressed themselves in symbols, not in deeds. Here battles were fought with smiles and insults, transgressions of etiquette and double entendres. A glance averted at the right moment could change the course of history. For years no blood had boiled.

"Uncle! Uncle!"

His nephew hoisted himself up to his full shapelessness, like a prophet.

"Uncle! Do you know how to write the word *thaut*?"

He pulled a piece of paper from a fold in his robe and shoved it under Wu's nose. On it was the character *emperor*. Well, fine, it was also the character for *thaut*.

Wu scrunched his wrinkled eyelids quizzically. He sensed this was a trick question, the sort of riddle the poet had loved as a child, and Wu had no desire to be tricked. In their language, the words *emperor* and *thaut* — the second signified some sort of half-forgotten mythical beast — were not pronounced the same, but for unknown reasons shared the same character. Everyone knew this, and because *thaut* appeared very rarely in ordinary speech, it did not cause the least confusion. No one gave it the slightest thought.

"See? See?" his nephew whispered, and his scar darkened with blood. "It was such a beautiful beast! It had golden horns and could fly through the air! It's an eternal shame. Is this how the elephant will end up?"

Wu shoved the paper away.

"I don't know what you have against elephants. The emperor enjoys being compared to them. Our emperor is quite fond of elephants."

"Well, I'll tell you," his nephew announced. He stood up, crumpled the sheet of paper, and threw it in the fire. "You I can tell, you won't betray me. In the time of one of the emperor's ancestors or, to be more precise, at the end of his grandfather's reign, the most common simile was that the emperor was like a thaut. Handsome as a thaut, wise as a thaut, and miraculous as a thaut. They went on and on, poets and others too. Then the emperor himself took the title Thaut."

"Where did you learn this?" Wu challenged him.

"I told you. At the bibliotheca."

"Who let you borrow poems from the reign of the emperor's ancestors?"

"I borrowed them on my own!" his nephew said in exasperation, as if unable to concede that there was anything odd about this. In truth, it was as shocking as borrowing the princess to study at home.

"No, I will not protect you! Never! I won't lift a finger for you!" Wu shouted.

His nephew bent over toward him secretively.

"I've discovered something no one else knows. Even my teacher didn't tell me about it. Once, you see, the word *thaut* was written differently. It had its own separate character!"

"Don't count on me once you're in hot water! I'll disown you! I should have done it long ago!"

"It was only when the emperor started calling himself Thaut that the two words came to be written with the same character. And at the same time this metaphor vanished from poetry, at once, instantly, as if the earth had swallowed it up! Don't you see? How could anyone still write: the emperor is like a thaut? Such a sentence would be pointless! Not only would it have been incomprehensible — it would have looked awfully clumsy as well!"

In spite of himself, Wu remembered that his nursemaid had once told him about the thaut. She swore she had seen it with her own eyes. If he remembered correctly, it was something like a chamois, but more clever, and able to fly. An elephant is much stronger.

"Then they began to compare the emperor to many other things. To the buffalo, to the sun, even — once! — to wheat. It was a great time for poetry!"

Oh no, Wu sighed inwardly. *Sin* and *sa* syllables. If I don't throw him out, he'll start reciting his latest brainchildren.

"But for fifty years now they've been babbling: the emperor's an elephant! The emperor's an elephant! They haven't learned from what happened before. You can't repeat anything too often, or it destroys itself. Back then it just happened, do you hear me! just happened to destroy the thaut. But this time it will destroy the emperor!"

Two things struck Wu during this tirade. First: what an unendearing person his nephew was! Second: the monastery superior would have made short work of him. The boy would have stopped his trickery, one two three!

"We think..." Excited, his nephew leaned right over to him and swallowed his final consonants, like a country boy. It was a bad habit picked up in the provinces. "We believe that the thaut never existed. That it's just a beast from old fables. But how do we know that, eh? What if it did exist, back then, what if it soared through the mountains and had golden horns? Who in God's name can say? What if it only disappeared when the emperor appropriated its name, whipped it out from under the thaut's nose, as if he had the right to it, as if it belonged to him? What if it had to disappear just because they were already so similar, there wasn't room in the world for both of them, and the thaut simply lost out?"

Wu's nephew thumped his fist against his knee.

"But the elephant is strong. He won't give way. Not the elephant!"

Wu still could not understand him. His nephew didn't even completely understand himself, because he was trying, tediously and without the necessary intellectual apparatus, to define a concept that had not yet come into existence. It was — let's call it — the concept of redundancy, and with it the allied concepts of innovation, informational esthetics, and possibly the exhaustibility of repertoire. Not only did these concepts not yet exist — there was not even a hint of the force which, in time, would coil in a loop around one of these matters and by sheer pressure compel the word into being.

Neither Wu nor his nephew could know that this would only come to pass in their part of the world a good two or three hundred years hence. But by then this palace would be overgrown with grass from end to end, and the great-grandson of the eastern gate's parrot would have died of homesickness in a foreign land no one in the palace had ever heard of. Both knew only this: that Wu's nephew was bitterly humiliated by his insignificance, and that he would never achieve fame — and he himself understood his own words less and less the more these feelings clogged them up.

"There are lots of elephants," the poet grinned cunningly. "They look quite plucky, don't you think, uncle? The last few weeks I've been going to watch them, observing them for hours."

Then he leaned over so far that his nose touched the clasps on Wu's chest, and Wu quickly took a step back. For years he had found physical intimacy unpleasant.

"Say 'the emperor's an elephant'!" his nephew pleaded passionately, but then, without waiting for an answer, he granted his own request: "The emperor's an elephant. The emperor's an elephant. The emperor's an elephant."

He waited a moment, as if listening for some subtle echo, and then shook his head:

"Nothing. It has no meaning anymore. There is no helping the emperor."

What he said was very simple. All the words he used were familiar to Wu. They weren't even mangled. But Wu did not understand them. Not only that — in the true sense of the word Wu had not even *heard* them. He had never thought of them and never considered anything even close to them. Later, in the time of the parrot's great-grandson, everyone would recognize them, and in three further generations they would be mute with age. But now they were mute with newness and Wu felt only their strangeness, a feeling so common for an old man that it told him nothing at all.

"Run along," he said. "Go home. I want to be alone now."

His nephew shuffled to his feet without protest. Suddenly he looked as expressionless as always, excepting the brief fever of his last speech. He gazed at length around the room, as if he had forgotten where the door was, and then said in a slight whine:

"Uncle! When will you be speaking with the Head Censor?"

Oh heavens, not again! Requests, petitions, mumbling, sniveling, muting of conversations as I come through the door, vanishing around corners, muttering behind my back, tugging at my sleeves —

"The Head Censor does not visit me!" he answered sharply.

"But couldn't you ... for old times' sake ..."

Suddenly Wu's blood boiled in his veins.

"Out!" he roared. "Scram!"

His nephew left; Wu did not see him out. He merely watched the young man's hunched back totter down the hall, and shook his head: how old he looks! At thirty-one I looked my thirty-one years, but I aged differently. There was a powerful current of youth, and a powerful current of old age surging against it, and their waters mixed with a roar, like a dam bursting. But him — he's a ditch full of dried-up mud.

He saw this image with absolute clarity, but he did not think it, and if he had had to describe his nephew's aging, he would not have found the word *water,* nor the word *ditch,* nor the word *current.*

When Wu entered the years of River (also known by the flowery name "midday mountain time," signifying a man's most powerful age, from forty to fifty), he created and discovered things with great ease. He was singularly ambitious and, thanks to his years in the monastery, remarkably disciplined. His inventiveness seemed bottomless.

The annual tradition of preparing a completely new chicken dish in honor of the emperor's birthday began at this time and for many years seemed completely unproblematic. He felt sure that he would have new ideas as long as he lived, and that it would always be in his power to create something that did not yet exist. Wu never presented his guests with the pinnacle of his art at any particular time. In the fermenting abundance of his inspiration, he offered one of many possible versions. He saw a geyser of creation inside himself, an inexhaustible source of innovation.

At first he had no inkling that *Wu's new chicken* would become a custom the whole empire would make its business. He did not even know that this era — this court, this land, this configuration of planets — worshiped tradition and misused it as a defense against its own unpredictability. Time hurtles forward, changes howl furiously at the boundaries of existence, tatters of the ages whirl in the winter wind, but one thing remains certain: year in, year out, on the emperor's birthday, dignitaries from all seven provinces gather to taste the new chicken of Master Wu.

Chicken was as integral to the emperor's birthday as the emperor himself. A ritual had developed around the tasting. Understandably, it was a great honor. The number of guests varied over the years, but had finally stabilized at twenty-two of the most powerful, who on that day were permitted only tepid water for breakfast, whom the heavens forbade to take lunch, and who, with the rising of the tiny autumn evening star, would finally receive a deep bowl containing five or six morsels of the new chicken. — Wu sometimes wondered whether he had succeeded in educating even one true gourmet who would esteem his art as only an expert could. Certainly he had terrorized those twenty-two people to such an extent that they slavered at the sight of the meal and did not speak until they had swallowed it.

For years Wu had no idea that, in addition to fame, this custom would earn him the title of chamberlain (to use Zenoic language), then later high chamberlain, and finally a nebulous position as one of the most powerful men in the empire, whose choleric shrieks over his skillets decided the fate of the court more surely than did any government petition.

Even Wu himself could not pinpoint when he had first lost his certainty that this year's recipe was completely different from the last. Perhaps it was the chicken with sesame, nine years ago. The sesame was in and of itself nothing novel. Its originality resided elsewhere: from the moment it hatched, the fledgling was fed a special mixture of herbs and grains soaked in hot infusions. It was incredibly ingenious and horrendously laborious, but even so, the result did not have a particularly innovative taste. The twenty-two guests consumed their portions with no less enthusiasm than before, which relieved Wu somewhat, while arousing in him an ill-focused feeling of contempt.

After all, there had been years that were incomparably better, more inventive, more distinctive. For instance, the clerical election year, when he had found a truly exceptional flavoring, known ever since as *I mourn you, lost love, my betrothed Li.*

(A note: these names were not Wu's doing; it was the emperor's literary office that thought them up, or more accurately classified them according to a classical key. The betrothed Li came from a fable, probably connected in some complicated way with the ruler's ancestry and thus especially in favor. But Wu himself did not know the story; it did not interest him and he had certainly never mourned her.)

Li owed her fame primarily to the fact that she was made from chickens not raised in their land. Wu had imported them from the south. Their long necks gave them a foreign air, true, but above all it was the masterly work Wu had done on them.

En route, several of Wu's chickens had expired from the tremendous heat. When he discovered this, a fearful rage overcame him, and he nearly beat to death the two laggards sauntering alongside the wagon. He was around fifty at the time, quick-tempered and quite brutal. However, after incalculable effort, hours suffering over the slow flame of enlightenment, he realized how to make use of the chickens' slightly spoiled tinge, and created a dramatically unusual dish.

It was then he learned the secret that as a deviation from the norm, a mistake serves just as well as anything. For a time he even flung himself into new experiments involving deliberately spoiled ingredients, and it must be said that, despite the morbid domain, he made some interesting discoveries.

Equally splendid was the year of the princess's engagement, when he had mixed the meat with the sweetly pungent juices of a local tree and made what was almost a dessert; and then the year (he could not remember which) when he froze the chicken until the pieces tinkled delicately in the bowls; and the year of chicken mousse whipped into a stormcloud. There were years when all he had to do was concentrate and an idea came as quickly as a cringing servant handing him a fork.

But for four years now his inspiration had lain mute. Five, actually, since the celebration was just around the corner. In five years he had not managed to find a new flavor.

There were moments when Wu thought he could not bear his impotence anymore. He did not give in to despair, because he was foremost a man of battle, but for the first time he was faced with the very worst: battle with the nonexistent. If he had seen a way forward, he would have followed it till he dropped, but for five years now it seemed he would drop right where he stood.

Many a time he had been willing to believe that the circle had closed, that there were no new flavors to find. Incidentally, there was a sect of astrologers, right in the palace, trumpeting the coming end of the world, "once all the words have been said," but the attitude toward them was one of silent reserve.

Wu still lived in the hope that once more the circle would break, that he would resist the grip of the nonexistent and find an herb that no mortal had ever tasted. He would get hold of something banal, something right in everyone's view, but hidden by the magic of its obviousness. Then the source would be forced to yield and to gush forth from the center of its being.

But the celebration was approaching, and as the sun rose he would stand over a pile of dirty bowls and then fall reluctantly into the fitful sleep of the elderly, of which he rarely remembered a thing.

There was a certain comfort in the fact that he did not really have to expend the effort. He knew full well that not one of the guests had a gustatory memory that could span thirty-six years.

Over time Wu had realized that it was he who was abnormal. But he had not yet fathomed that aside from his exceptional culinary imagination, he was a rather ordinary person. His tongue was a miraculous floating island in a sea of superficial education, unrefined sensibility, and quite unexceptional intelligence. He was like those feeble-minded twins from Košice who can multiply five-digit numbers in their heads but will never understand how a toilet flushes. Or — going further back in history! — like the Paris garage attendant who speaks thirty languages fluently but only reads comics and invoices, because his spirit reaches no farther than the metal grating of his garage. — Wu knew that he could offer any of the last thirty-five chickens without anybody recognizing them, but that option still seemed impermissible.

All it took to make him soak his deathbed in sweat was to remember how last year he had stood all day in the Meadow Pavilion, staring for hours into the water. The low, heavy sky turned gray toward night, and the raging river carried with it wrecks, carcasses, beaten trees, and drooping clusters of water narcissus.

Here is how this ignoble story unfolded. He had announced chicken stuffed with stalks of river greens, but the day before the celebration the river flooded and the plans had to be abandoned. Everyone understood, and no one even raised an eyebrow. Wu alone knew why specifically river greens, which, incidentally, were sour and unpalatable. Eight days before — eight days in which he had depopulated the hen-house, like Herod, slaughtering a generation of chickens — a certain foreigner had come uninvited to the court. More precisely, it was a suspicious-looking friend of his nephew's, most likely in flight from some arm of the law, who in the dead of night had begged Wu for shelter. He said that floods had begun on the Five Rivers and that whole villages had fled wailing into the mountains. Early the next morning he disappeared without a good-bye and no one ever saw him again.

Wu had lived long enough to know how to seize the day. With considered trepidation, he announced his river-greens plan the morning after the boy took off. Then there was no alternative but to wait. He did not know who would come out on top, he or time.

He stood for hours, eyes fixed on the horizon. For the first time in his life he burned the porridge. He did not speak for four days.

At least the heavens granted him this one belated favor. The flood came a day early. The celebration ground to a halt, the whole court was thrown into terror, an evacuation was planned. On a day of impatient surrogate celebration, Wu left the palace early and spent the whole day by himself in the Meadow Pavilion, until the empress herself sent a message, telling him to forget about the stupid chicken and to come make her a handful of beer-roasted almonds.

One such memory is more than enough, and the year was again mercilessly drawing toward autumn. The festivities began tomorrow. There was nowhere to call for help. Wu's "where"

— more than just a place inside him — had vanished with the same inaudible treachery as his inventiveness.

When Wu was very young, he had been a large hungry container the whole world poured itself into. Later (around fifty, when he was proudest, fiercest, and also unexpectedly powerful, which took some getting used to) he had formed the impression that he and the world were equal partners. It was a matter of his will what and whom he opened up to, and he would take the first move, extending his hand, accepting things rationally and voluntarily. But now the end had come. There was nothing to contain. He had had what there was to have. He was living off himself alone. The world's nozzle had gradually shut off. These days no one gave him anything at all.

His outside world had narrowed to the smallest possible dimensions, the mere shell of a corporeal body which moved with him through space. But recently even this had been further constrained. He never left the kitchen, banquet hall, and the two adjoining corridors. In the day as he slept, at night as he paced from corner to corner like a wild beast, he was plagued by the imminence of his fate. Day after day, time lost its patience. The world was as cramped as a small shoe. In addition, Wu was extremely nearsighted, although no one even suspected it, and thus he had learned to live in the immediate, ever more strictly attuned only to what was within his reach.

They had already painted the great staircase vermilion in honor of the emperor's birthday. Wu locked the kitchen and transferred the burden of daily work onto his staff. Once or twice he sent out for spices. He had them bring large quantities of ice. He requested a bucket of river sand and a tiny vessel of white ointment used only for cosmetic purposes.

In the final three days nobody saw him. A cloud of black smoke would occasionally pour from his windows, and then a cloud of white smoke. Bowls were frequently heard smashing against the wall.

*

Night had begun. Wu was tossing out a greasy ladle. The basket by the door — as always at this time — overflowed with similar utensils. Suddenly there was a quiet knock.

With a glass stick slightly flattened at one end, Wu scooped up some red porridge. Then he closed his eyes. He had heard the knocking, but still did not react. It had been many years since anyone visited him at night, and there was no reason suddenly to start believing in ghosts.

Carefully, he wiped the porridge onto the middle and, a second later, onto the tip of his tongue. For a moment he stood with his tongue stuck straight out at attention and imbibed the waves of his breath, then began sibilantly to roll them back up. Just as the taste poured over his upper palate like a carpet of sparkling colors, someone banged on the door again.

Freeze, Wu thought. Freeze like a lizard on a greensward. There's no one I want to see. No one has the right to take away my final night.

Quietly he rinsed out his mouth and, with a hunter's concentration, set off on the trail of the taste still quivering on his palate. He had often done this. Mornings would find him walking from wall to wall, mouth agape like a gargoyle, flicking his tongue to dispell the last impression, which often slipped to the very edge of pain.

He knew himself exceptionally well. The monastery had given him a thorough and — except for a couple of insignificant trifles — an anatomically correct understanding of his body, but he knew the worn honeycomb of his tongue best of all. He and his tongue, in fact, had embarked on a strange dual relationship, as when the ego distances itself from one of its parts to be able to experience it better — even at the price of having that part abuse its deceptive autonomy and take on its own life. It was a relationship that could take over one's soul or nature, a relationship full of emotions, naive guardianship, anger, and lack of understanding.

There might have been happier moments in Wu's life, but none were more fulfilling than these minutes spent between shimmering shadows, when he stood in taut concentration, scraping his tongue against his eager gums, trying with all his might to understand. To feel, distinguish, know, assimilate. And again he would set out on his usual route from wall to stove, his fiery tongue flicking out of his mouth like some frenzied divinity.

"Wu?" said a hesitant voice from the darkness. And then again: "Wu?"

Wu froze. Something in his saurian stillness moved slightly. In the whole court, in the whole palace and the whole wide empire, there was no one aside from the shades of the dead who was allowed to call him by name alone. As he raised the latch, he sucked back his sharp saliva with a hiss.

"I knew," said his guest, making a gesture of greeting with one narrow palm, "that I would find you here at this time, Wu."

Wu stood silently, his hands in his sleeves, watching the empire's Head Censor fold up the material of his robe with precise, academically spare movements and then sit down facing him. For a few minutes both old men remained silent.

Outside an angry beak squawked. In the darkness there were many sounds Wu did not recognize. The sentence the censor had just spoken was the first one between them in thirty-three years.

"Wu," the censor eventually said — impersonally, as if relaying an unclear message — "tomorrow your nephew will be executed."

⁂

The role of this imperial censor in the history of the empire's poetry — and, in a way, of the whole world's poetry — was far from insignificant. In his fertile years he ruled his language's marketplace. History traditionally pigeonholes him as "a co-founder of subjective poetry," but that "co-" is deceptive, for the others who co-founded it missed our censor by hundreds of miles and dozens of years.

Now the censor slowly slipped his hand underneath his robe. He drew out a sheet of paper.

"He entered this in the emperor's birthday contest."

His face was in its way perfect — so perfect that it is hard to report what sort of face it was. It was so cultivated as to be a sort of abstraction: not degenerate or decadent, but an ineffable harmony of features, a small hollow of silence at the very summit of its consummation.

Wu took the sheet from the censor. It was scribbled from margin to margin in a familiar hand — careless but without lightness, illegible without grace. He raised the paper to his eyes and felt ashamed, with the preposterous vanity of old men who have not grown old together. He saw instantly that it was some sort of trick. The first stanza ran as follows:

The Emperor
is an emperor
is an emperor
is an emperor.

The second:

The Emperor
is like an emperor
who is like an emperor
who is like an emperor
that is emperor.

The third stanza is more or less untranslatable, for the construction governing the words *emperor* and *emperor* can be translated either as *nothing but* or *precisely such* or also *most highly similar* and a few other variants. In older translations we sometimes find the possibility ... *he and only he!* and in the contemporary form of the language (in what is left of these etymological seeds) this construction confirms the complete identity of two mathematical elements.

The fourth stanza is the most chaotic and can only be understood in a logical and linguistic trance. It says, roughly:

If the Emperor,
who is emperor
and likewise is like an emperor
and is nothing but an emperor
(he and only he!)

were not emperor
who is like an emperor
and nothing else
than emperor himself,
there would be no emperor.

"What is it supposed to mean?" Wu said without even raising his eyes. "Has he gone mad?"

"Oh no ... I do not think it is exactly that," the censor replied in that featureless tone that never conveyed more than he wished.

"Then why bring it to me?" Wu burst out in annoyance, fixing his eyes on the censor. Even the censor did not know about Wu's poor vision; he did not realize that the gaze fixed so directly on him saw only an indistinct outline, and that it was this which gave Wu such a firm sense of security. Wu was aware of the secret power of the nearsighted: this was how he stared at the servants when the bowls weren't hot enough, and at the princess when she tasted her food.

The other old man responded with a shapely curve of his fingers, which in the language of gestures meant *I defer to you,* as if indicating that he could certainly answer, but was giving Wu a chance to come to it himself. Wu knew this maneuver all too well from years past. Two ancient tricks dissolved mutely into one another, and for a while there was quiet. When they finally spoke, their words came together.

"The emperor is most ungracious just now," the censor said.

And Wu: "Does my nephew know?"

The censor shook his head. Then he added unexpectedly:

"That's why I'm here. Explain it to me."

"Me? What's there for me to explain?" Wu tossed the paper onto the floor. His eyebrows bristled like blades of grass.

Without even knowing why he was so furious, he felt his old anger welling up inside.

"Why me?"

"I hoped," the censor said soothingly, "I hoped you'd know something about it. That's the only reason I dared disturb you."

"I don't know anything!" Wu snapped. Acrid smoke rose, burning, through a crack in his memory. "It's mishmash, no head or tail. It's nonsense!"

"I do not recommend executions," the censor replied, his laconic gesture of release indicating utter resignation, "and it is not in my power to overturn the sentence. But I would like to understand for myself something so ... so... "

He hesitated and then added tentatively:

"Something so ... exceptional?"

As to the censor's role in the history of poetry, he is among those who are, as they say, a step ahead of their time. The censor achieved this in a very strange way. He stepped ahead of his time without that time even noticing it was being stepped over. The censor's genius lay in the inconspicuousness of his actions. His adroit strategy tamed the world's vicissitudes and inconspicuously overturned the course of an era.

The poetry of the temporally bounded enclave that spanned the old men's birth consisted of purely objective military epics. A more diligent analysis than ours would reveal its song-like format, its stereotypical plot schemes and, most of all, its marked poverty. The same heroic fragments predominate time after time, and the poems are as alike as two peas in a pod. For generations no individual spirit had come forth.

It would not be precisely true to say that the censor played the same role in his time as Sappho did in Greece, for he formed a channel from one style into another and was king in both. He established himself in official poetry, even as a young man imposing on it a certain pervasive lightness without distinguishing himself from it in any special way. Only when he had made his name, when he had become a significant partici-pant in the imperial Word, did an unheard-of note begin to creep into his work: private life and emotion.

At first it mimicked existing traditions so precisely that no one even noticed it. Its quantity increased only gradually, with a diplomacy usually reserved for altering word order in government documents — but suddenly, without that generation's ever expecting it, they found the censor's *tone* had become the voice of the century.

Today, when, through none of our own doing, we understand better, we know that the censor was truly a great poet, and prefigured an age in poetry probably fifty times longer than the age he himself attained — which was quite advanced. His poems, especially those of his *midday mountain,* are widely read and critiqued to this day. Even now the best of them can, in their depth and fervency, stand up to the highest achievements of all future times, and placed next to them even a nineteenth-century *poète maudit* seems a bit too heavily starched.

But the most wonderful part was that the censor's contemporaries did not know about it; the censor did not disturb or insult them, as such harbingers tend to do. The change from the monotonous racket of military campaigns to hysterical confessional trembling is so leisurely that the enlightened modern reader studying the censor's work cannot avoid the impression of a clear plan and exceptionally adroit staging. A historian of our time, a young Swede, aptly called it "ecstasy by flowchart."

"Wu, speak, please — if you can, of course," the censor gently pleaded.

At fifty the poet in him had fallen silent; he obtained a government post and the track of his poetry suddenly disappears with no explanation.

The birdcalls grew louder; outside it was deepest night. Midnight flared down from the heavens in a twinkling of lights. Laboriously and against his own will, Wu dug from his memory snippets of their absurd conversation.

"Did the boy visit you today?" the censor asked, but it did not sound very much like a question.

"Why do you ask if you already know?"

"I haven't had you watched, I'm thinking it through. Wu, there's not much time before dawn. The execution will be secret, so as not to disturb the celebration. Did the boy tell you anything about his poem?"

In a tremor of anger Wu felt himself nodding to the censor. He tried to prevent it; he did not want to comply, and he hated the feeling that the censor was concealing something from him. Arrogance, peremptory pride — once again he knows best! It was always thus, always — and thirty-three years hadn't changed anything at all.

"He's gotten it into his head that the emperor will disappear," Wu snorted. The censor's placid face immediately tensed.

"Disappear? Why?"

For a moment he resembled an old bird, a slender, withered raptor.

"Because there are too many elephants in our poetry," Wu answered. His masticatory muscles tensed in anger at having to repeat such drivel.

"Go on! What else did he say? Go on!"

The censor leaned over in his chair, and suddenly his elaborate elderly deferentiality gave way to the aggressiveness of a secret imperial lord. His handsome face regained its shape.

Wu had always been far removed from the world of poetry. Although he had been forced to live his whole life at its legally sanctioned heart, it had never held great interest for him. It is fair to say he took note of it only once the censor had initiated the ingenious inch-by-inch shift from propaganda songs to the torment of self-reflection. And strange as it sounds, Wu belonged to that scant handful who noticed the difference. What's more, the change astounded him far more than it astounds us today, from the heights of our foreshortened omniscience of all those years to come.

"The thaut. He went on about the thaut."

"And then?"

"As if I know! That the thaut used to have its own character."

The tall functionary suddenly stood up. With surprising agility he strode over to the stove and grabbed the ash-rake from the wall. While Wu spoke, while he dredged fragments and snatches from his memory, in rapt attention the censor sketched word after word on the dirty tiles.

"Quiet!" he abruptly silenced the chef. "Not another word. Let me think."

He tapped the rake and then squatted. Pained, Wu stared at the narrow back, at the censor in all his imperial majesty, robed in gold from head to toe, crouched in a position Wu associated only with servants, or with little girls, who could toy with things this way for days on end.

Suddenly the censor laughed. It was a laugh full of wonder and distress. Then he shook his head and put back the rake.

"Wu," he said politely, "excuse me, I'll be leaving now. But I'd like to know: where does your nephew sleep?"

*

When Wu was a bit over forty (he was slightly the elder of the two old men) the censor's existence struck him like a lightning bolt to the head. It happened in late spring, one luminous evening. It is relevant that Wu already thought he was past his peak.

It is true that, from a certain perspective, the censor temporarily became his "number one," despite the fact that Wu never felt toward him any love or affection in the true sense of the words, or even closeness or trust. But still, thanks to the censor (or rather: in the grip of his emotional force field) Wu experienced these feelings more deeply and passionately than ever before.

Long ago, when the censor's thunderous confessional whisper first resounded in the world's Word, Wu knew as little as could be known about poetry. He had never had the slightest need for the medium of words, and treated poetry with the indifferent attitude typical of masters in other professions. He had a simplistic, if by and large correct view of poetry as a secondary accompaniment to music and, of course, as the history of the empire. Wu always vastly preferred wandering tellers of fables and outlaw stories, which no longer fell into that category.

When quite by accident he later heard one of the censor's more intimate poems (he remembers it to this day: it was a clear evening, the sun was pale, the censor was smoking, and the smoke from his mouth rose into the olive branches), he was shaken to the depths of his soul.

The poem that struck him so was not intellectually complex and today would be dismissed as banal. It unobtrusively expressed surprise at a common fact: namely, that there was a single encounter, never repeated, which the poet could not forget, while in his heart's memory people he saw every day were far less meaningful. It was essentially just the flip side of the German wordplay *einmal ist keinmal, aber zweimal ist dreimal* — "once is never, but twice is thrice." Emotional life is exactly the opposite, as we know. There *einmal* is a relatively high card and singularity is the gate to eternity.

(Incidentally, a further note: a few years later, when Wu no longer knew him, the censor finally arrived at the celebration of the sovereign *never,* at the troubadors' *amor d'onques,* which sings the praises of unrequited love. *That which has not happened* always has a slightly unfair advantage over reality. It is hard to say whether the censor knew this from his own experience. It could have merely been logical speculation, in which his beloved leitmotif reached its most extreme point.)

But the poem Wu heard that day was not this far along. Formally it was modest. It revealed the fatal *einmal* in a traditional form full of flowers, meteorological phenomena, and melancholy evening sounds.

Wu was astounded. He was promiscuous by nature, as is common among such sensual beings, and he was also impatient. He had never understood why (in the language of his scullions) he so quickly lost interest in every woman and why repetition deprived physical love of all savor. It was that fateful *einmal* that made the strongest impression; after it, everything else seemed shallow. He was astounded that someone else could feel the same way. He had never spoken of his *einmal* — a thin, middle-aged woman, long ago, when he had trekked across the desert in his youth — to anyone, even to himself. And suddenly someone had said out loud what had happened to Wu, and had said it precisely, rhythmically, openly.

Wu did not understand how anyone could name that mute gust of wind, and not only name it, but broadcast it. It was not chastity or introversion that bewildered him; he was simply and methodically amazed at the shattering of a concept — here, presumably, the concept of poetry. Someone had jumped the hedge of his heart, penetrated his gravitational field. The cook was overcome by shock.

But once that first astonishment had passed, it was replaced by a much more subtle amazement. Wu discovered that he could identify, more or less, with the majority of the censor's poems, which he only now began to notice. It seemed to him that the censor, by some sleight of hand, could look right into his blindly tumbling soul and then willfully toy with it out loud.

Inexperienced as he was, Wu took every word as an authentic expression of the censor's feelings and was startled by their great similarity. Yet it is worth noting the single, characteristically intractable mistake the impatient cook was making. It is, by the way, an exceedingly common mistake, and even today various psychologies have foundered on it.

Wu had had a rare experience: an alien inner space had been opened to him, one which he had till then been unaware of, but he was only tentatively getting his bearings in it. He accepted it quite simply — we could even say *flatly,* at the expense of its multilayeredness. Wu had erroneously let himself believe that every hidden feeling he found in this other ego had to be made of the same substance. He did not know that hiddenness does not by any means entail depth, that secrets can be utterly superficial. Lacking experience in the affairs of the soul, Wu was fascinated to hear the censor speak of things that were not commonly discussed — which was, incidentally, the censor's primary contribution to literary history. The more the censor's work enthralled him, the more he came to believe that the two of them were a single being. The other man was by some magic speaking for him and, like the wind, stealing the words from his mouth.

Wu put himself into close contact with the censor. With persistence he became the censor's constant companion, in order to get to the heart of the matter. Wu saw the censor as some sort of freak of nature. He studied him like a spice box.

The censor (we will let him keep this title for clarity's sake, but back then he was not yet censor; he obtained that post only once his productive days were past) was a tall, polished, somewhat coolly attractive man. A ring of reserve surrounded him; inside it he had no real friends. He was not married and did not conduct "affairs." The censor accepted Wu's aggressive affections with kindness and a monotonous politeness, and in time he even found a certain pleasure in his debates with the master chef.

This not too close friendship lasted about three years. After all that time Wu was not a step nearer his goal. His tenacity came to nothing. Who is this man? How does he know what I know and yet don't know? And why him?

The more Wu saw the censor, the more the man disturbed him. He simply could not reconcile that restrained — one could even say British — exterior with the fevered cry of his poetry. They spent hours together on the covered terraces, idly gossiping just so as not to lapse into silence. In his work Wu was accustomed to step-by-step analysis; at one point he secretly focused on one after another of the censor's characteristics — his face, tastes, way of speaking — and delved into them with a persistence he had never before applied to another person. But the censor's eyes were expressionless, his hands calm as they poured the wine, and his tastes temperately indifferent.

By the third year he felt the censor was deliberately deceiving him. The further this current of introspection carried him, the more he came to believe that while he conducted his detailed study of the censor, the censor was doing the same to him. In each new poem he found a piece of himself and countless times erroneously ascribed to himself the poem's feelings and states. He experienced an entire range of emotions never before imagined, and he was quick to appropriate each of them, like a hypochondriac does with the symptoms of diseases. In the final analysis, poets everywhere can thank this egocentricity and its uncontrollable tendency toward error for the fact that we tolerate poetry's existence at all.

"How did you think up that poem?" he would turn on the censor during their early evening meetings. "Who were you thinking about? What kind of mood were you in when you wrote it?"

Wu posed the censor questions that are heard all the time on television. He rousted them forcefully from time's womb. The answers that most of today's artists prefabricate as an integral part of their work were at the time beyond anyone's concern. The creator as subject was beside the point. Wu's insistence came across as slightly vulgar.

"This?" the censor would answer with a smirk. "I don't even know. I can't remember."

"When did you write it?" Wu would not be put off.

"Yesterday."

"All at once?"

"No. Before supper and after."

"And what did you have for supper?" Wu would persist, growing louder and louder, until the servants on the terraces stopped to look.

"Duck."

"With what?"

"Something green. Broad beans, perhaps? No, probably string beans."

"What did you think about during supper?"

"I don't know."

"Why not?"

At some point Wu's desire to understand the censor turned into an obsession. He tracked him like a hunter. Day after day he prized intimate details out of him, longed to lay bare his heart, and still failed to get even the most everyday confidences so easily shared among his cooks.

"You have to know what you were thinking! It was yesterday evening! Any idiot knows what happened yesterday!" Wu would shout.

"Aha, now I know. I was thinking about the fact that the west wing is the oldest part of the entire palace. They should really get the roof repaired. The administrator isn't forward-looking enough to anticipate the autumn rains," was his exhaustive, obliging, and empty answer.

As the sunlight over the terrace gradually faded, Wu would wander deeper into ever more inconclusive interrogation. Finally he would stalk off, full of anger, each time bewildered that a poem created not an hour after this tiresome chatter could be a crowning achievement of refined insight and an astounding inner likeness.

At that age Wu was already quite powerful and dangerously irascible. He ruled the fate of hundreds and took hard the feeling that the censor was making fun of him. One day, using a minor palace conflict as a pretext, Wu shouted at him that he'd had enough of his supercilious glances. The censor gave him a kindly smile. In the grip of an insane rage, Wu grabbed a bowl of boiling water and hurled it at the censor's feet. The puddle soaked their boots, which were made of the same thin material. It got him no further with the censor.

*

One day, a month or so after that evening of rage and shards, a short episode occurred which again changed the course of Wu's life.

He was swimming in the pond. It was morning, a bright, early autumn; the water was warm and full of tiny greenery. Wu swam quickly toward the sun, taking pleasure in his small, stocky body. He was so used to thinking of the censor at such moments that his mind had created a sort of feedback loop, checking every impression with the censor's imagined stream of thoughts.

Even now, as he swam, he posed himself the thousandth version of one and the same question: how would the censor feel about this? How would he — who is not me, and yet in some startling way is — perceive this motion, this meeting of water and skin, the glow of September sun on scalp; how would he see the mountain on the horizon, the white cloud? (The censor never went to the pond; he probably did not even know how to swim, but Wu experimented assiduously with every situation, hoping that one day, in one of them, he would find an answer.)

He glanced at the tips of his clasped hands, which surged rapidly forward. And suddenly, as he caught sight of his fingers, unusually pale beneath the water, slightly changed by the refracted light, seaweed wrapped around his ring-finger — suddenly he was outside himself, and outside everything he had ever known. His body dragged him toward the bottom like a weight. He looked up at a mountain towering over him, so alien that it was almost not a mountain. He breathed in as if someone were forcing air into his mouth.

That was all. It lasted only a moment and there is nothing more to say. But during those several seconds Wu realized once and for all that the censor was the censor and Wu was Wu — he and only he! — and that all his efforts were in vain, for nothing he could learn from the censor would ever be anything other than Wu.

We cannot rule out a purely physical origin for this feeling: for instance, a change in equilibrium, which can certainly occur while swimming. Wu tried many times that morning to recapture it, swimming back and forth across the pond, observing himself with great care, but the feeling never returned.

From that day forth he never called on the censor again. The interest that had exhausted him for three years had suddenly subsided. The circle was full and the time bounded by his forty-second and forty-fifth years came to a close.

The palace, of course, noticed this change and ascribed it to a meaningless intrigue unfolding at the time. The censor himself silently accepted the turn of events and probably thought the same, but Wu's life was so marked by that moment of estrangement that he was unable to imagine what the censor might have thought of it, and instead put him out of his head as best he could.

*

Three hours after the censor left, Wu was still in the kitchen, working. He was searching. There was no sense now trying to sleep. It was still as dark as in the very depths of night, but Wu knew that at this time of year dawn came more quickly than an axe blow.

He worked as if entranced. Time dwindled like the smoldering logs. The night was drawing to a close. The confrontation he had been waiting for these thirty-three years and which had slipped by only minutes ago had deprived time of all elasticity. Haste possessed him.

Angry and headstrong, alone, without his servants' help, he lifted giant bowls and stoked the stove. It was nearly the death of him. The meat tongs fell on his hand and made his knuckles bleed, but he did not even notice. He pushed time aside.

Wu worked differently than ever before. He stopped relying on external aids. On sauces, spices, fruits, and additives, on all those glittering cosmetics of flavor. He turned to the very fundaments of his art. He focused his attention on the operations he performed every day, on each process, however simple. He investigated the element of fire, the element of water in braising. The hiss from under the pan, the steam on the ceiling, the hot gust from the oven doors. For ten minutes he stood motionless and, eyes closed, fingered the bottom of one of the pots. He penetrated the most primitive components of creation.

It was the most potent hour of the night, the last before dawn. Wu worked like a man possessed. He was certain he would find something. He no longer tasted. Taste was secondary. The meat's very consistency came alive in his hands. It hardened, softened, took on an unnatural brittleness; its very structure gave way, collapsing into other forms of being, and the chicken was already as little chicken as smoke in the sky is a tree in flames. Just before the potent hour gave way to morning, Wu knew that he had found it.

He was putting away his forks in the gray of morning when someone began to knock gently on the door. For a moment his heart stopped. In a lightning vision he admitted the censor, conducted a long and fateful conversation with him — and then opened the door to see his nephew standing there on the other side.

The poet was shaking. He was wet and bloated. Before Wu could recover, the young man had slipped inside like a mouse.

"What do you think you're doing? Out!" Wu roared.

Wu clenched his fists tight. Pain reminded him of his raw knuckles, but he no longer remembered why they hurt.

"Uncle! Uncle!" the boy squealed. Stiffly he pressed his knees together. "They want to kill me! I'm going to be executed!"

The boy's lower lip trembled. Just don't start to whimper, Wu thought. He was dead tired. The idea of tears on his nephew's fleshy and always slightly lubricious lips repelled him. Now, after hours straining his imagination to study the substance's essences and flavors, he would not be able to stand it. He closed his eyes and held his breath.

"What do you want?" Wu asked.

"Executed!" his nephew yelped. "They're digging a pit beyond the ramparts! It's raining! They'll bury me in mud!"

"I repeat: what do you want?"

Wu stamped his foot. The young man instantly sobered up. He blinked, shook his shoulders, and said quite forthrightly:

"Clothes."

"What kind?"

"Doesn't matter. A servant girl's, maybe."

"Who sent you here?"

Wu's nephew sniffled loudly. "The censor. He said you'd know."

In the grayness Wu nodded slightly. The ties binding me to others in this world are fewer day by day, he realized. Other people's paths still cross behind my back, but each day even those are further away.

"There are clothes in the alcove," the young man added pragmatically. "And a cap. And some kind of ... basket or something."

Wu sighed. It was part of his old age, of that empty, ever narrowing path, that he could not even remember anything about his servant girl. He groped blindly around the alcove, feeling various sorts of things whose existence he would rather leave be. The minute he ceased to need her each evening, she simply melted into nothingness — and any clothes she did not need were already in such an abyss of oblivion that he probably would not have noticed them if they were right under his nose. Finally he felt a soft material.

"Did the Head Censor have a message for me?"

"No."

When Wu returned to the kitchen, his nephew was lounging

on the chair, looking as if he did not know he was to be executed that morning.

"That crook!" the poet announced, his voice full of rancor. "That stuffed old mummy!"

Wu closed his eyes again. He did not want to watch his nephew disrobe. He was utterly exhausted and experiencing a strange feeling: he wanted to go to sleep.

"He's an ignoramus, " the youth continued. "An imbecile. He acted so clever!"

The poet drew in his greasy lips and mewed in an old man's voice:

"'Too soon, young man, too soon. This age isn't ripe for you' — he's a moron!"

Wu did not even realize he had fallen asleep. For an illusory moment he was ten again and a small, frightened monk ... creeping through the leaves and grubbing in the wet soil with his fingers —

"I can't stand him!" his nephew mumbled through the clothing's material. "His stench is everywhere. He's crawling with maggots, but won't let anyone else near the trough. It's not like anyone reads his doggerel. If I ever come back, it'll be to spit on his grave!"

The youth said this with the gloomy resolution of the swarthy southern prophets of old. The end of the world is nigh, they most often claimed. But also: the sun will grow cold, the universe will fall into small black holes — and this strange, age-old fascination with the end had always found them hordes of worshipers.

Wu's nephew pulled on a shapeless gray cap.

"Well, Uncle, I'm off."

And then suddenly he burst into caustic laughter:

"And he's still frightened of me! He's scared witless. I know he is! And the best thing is, he doesn't even know why!"

Wu woke up. The young man stood in the doorway in the servant girl's clothes, looking particularly unappealing. The insipid shapelessness of his sex, his age, his character, and the fate that had marked him forever was only heightened by those bedraggled rags, hurriedly fastened and lopsided.

"He told me to go around the pond. Promised to call off the guards."

Wu rubbed his warm, dry eyes. His nephew casually opened his arms to embrace him. The old man shrank back.

"Run along," he said, exhausted.

His nephew had already stepped across the threshold. But the youth turned around.

"I am the only one, remember," he whispered deliriously, "who could have saved the emperor ... and everything. Just me, who is myself and no one else. I and only I!"

"It's dawn," Wu answered.

The morning fog seeped through the partly closed door. Wu moved closer to the oven. He did not even watch the boy totter off and disappear into the gray rain. He forgot him so completely that the young man vanished from his life long before reaching the pond.

Wu carefully brushed off the hot ash. He removed the lid. The substance steaming in the pot did not in the least resemble meat. It was pulpy, shiny white, broken here and there by a vivid pink streak. If his nephew had returned at that moment, Wu would have thought it was the servant girl come to wash the dishes.

*

The palace shone. Lights burned in both its halls. The main impression the majority of guests took away that night was luminosity. Several small children, who were allowed to roam the hall during the festivities, would remember, even sixty years and two sadistic wars later, the gold-tinged glow, the thousands of candles, and the iridescent smoke up near the ceiling.

By the time the emperor arrived, the festivities were almost over. The emperor was an old man, and celebrations exhausted him. He was only a winged golden wisp waving half-asleep over a cosseted empire, dreaming the occasional short, pale dream.

All the winning poems had been recited. Now a small ephebe — the son of a court lady, probably the emperor's bastard child — took the stand and began to read, or rather to chant, the one that had received first prize. He had a strange voice, as tiny as if it were made of foam, and the voice and poem matched exquisitely.

Wu walked among the tables and checked the settings. The twenty-two bowls were already sitting on polished trays; there was a white cloth over each bowl and a waiter was placing sprigs of jasmine on them.

Wu stopped. The poem was rippling down the usual stairway of *sin – sa* syllables like a multicolored runner. Dominating it, as expected, was yet another elephant. This time it was an almost supernatural one, with diamond eyes, golden hair, and a set of classical enchantments skillfully woven into its elephantine anatomy.

This poem is simply beautiful, Wu thought, without the slightest sense of enchantment. "Perfect!" the old empress announced loudly, and in doing so completely expressed his feelings.

When the poem came to an end, there was an appreciative murmur. Everyone bent as if beneath a strong wind, and in their tiny bows to the emperor, empress, and Mr. Hayo, the winner, they made their satisfaction plain.

Finally came the time for the meal. By now the twenty-two bowls were on the tables. Wu could not help noticing as here and there someone tried inconspicuously to sniff or to ascertain with a brief touch at least whether it was to be a hot or cold dish. An unexpected disquiet seized him. Far away, in the gallery, a spoon fell, and the chilling reverberation of its tone raced sharply down his spine.

It was strange. He had lived a tumultuous life. He had destroyed many people and saved others. Nothing had passed him by. He had known hatred, passion, revenge, power and glory. There were many bodies he had known from inside and at least *einmal* he had experienced a moment of love. Wu had walked through that boisterous throng of people, been covered in their stigmas. But now, at the end, the only people he noticed were those twenty-two utterly alien beings, of whom — other than the emperor, the empress and the Head Censor — he barely knew a one. In most cases, their death would not have given him a moment's pause, and yet now he breathed their breath and suffered their impatience. In a moment, the last great work of his life would vanish into their hidden senses.

Finally the drum rolled. The headwaiters threw back the cloths. The hall fell quiet like footsteps on moss as the guests placed the first morsel into their ceremonially cleansed mouths. The quiet lasted a moment before the whispers began. It was not common practice to speak during this meal, but now a whirlwind of amazement swept round the hall.

Wu saw the guests raise their heads. His ready pride swelled up inside him. He knew full well why the amazement: the substance they had put in their mouths was so utterly unlike meat that tiny scandals were being played out in the delicate interplay of their senses. They had experienced all the world's tastes, but inevitably conveyed by the soft tissue of meat. What crunched between their teeth was fresh pulp.

"Master!" the old empress shouted energetically. She tapped her spoon against her necklace. "Where is that man?"

Wu smiled. He did not try to restrain the waves of proud delight washing over him. The lights blinded him as he strode into the hall, and it was only by memory that he found his way to the fat dowager.

"Listen here, boy," she said reproachfully, "what is this supposed to be?"

"I don't know what you mean," Wu modestly replied. Delays on both sides would only heighten the impression.

"This thing! This is what I mean!" she snapped, poking her finger into her supper. "It's trickery! Sleight of hand! Is this supposed to be chicken?"

From anyone else — even the emperor — it would have been unconscionable, but this powerful, gold-adorned idol had a right to her quirks.

"It most certainly is chicken, O mighty empress." Wu spoke firmly, as if on stage. He noticed fleetingly that the emperor had closed his eyes and was fumbling around the dish with his spoon turned round side up.

"It has been prepared using special, completely new methods in order to celebrate the greatest of all emperors!"

"M-hm," said the empress, loudly enough so that half the

court could hear it. Then she leaned over and pulled a ring off her finger.

"Your hand!" she ordered, tapping imperiously on the table. She placed the ring on Wu's bony middle finger. It was far too large for Wu to wear, but he quickly bent his finger like a claw and with a bow retreated from the table.

Everyone stared decorously at this act of heavenly favor, and as if the empress's naughtiness had been a signal to relax, everyone suddenly began to speak and bow in Wu's direction.

"A miracle! In our age of reason — a miracle!" shouted Mr. Hayo, apparently believing that with fame he could relax his standards a bit.

"The crow got the golden feather!" another poet said. "The tear has turned into a pearl!"

In front of everyone Wu finally uncovered his bowl and placed a morsel on his tongue. His pride glowed like never before. It was not the youthful pride of an initiate (no crown of promise weighed him down anymore); it was the sonorous pride of departure. Extinction's mighty vibrations pervaded the entire hall. Wu knew that, for a few moments, he had called into existence something no one would ever make again, which even now was disappearing from the face of the earth. In a timeless flash he had wrenched his portion from unreality, defied the inertia of all things — and unreality would swallow it along with him.

"You'd never believe it was meat!" someone remarked in an absurdly deep voice, but it was clear that he was being respectful.

Wu devoted himself to tasting this first morsel. As if meditating, he concentrated all his senses on it. He marshaled his attention — the way his superior had taught him, poking

Wu in the back with his short cane — guiding it in from the outside, through the gates of sense, where it anchored firmly in his mouth, and then he began to relentlessly pulverize the stimulus.

The impression the meat gave was very strange. You would never believe you were eating meat. You would swear you had a freshly cut stalk on your tongue. Neither would you find it particularly tasty. Just surprising. Its taste was weak, hidden by that moist vegetable frangibility. Its tones were strange. Wu expertly rolled the morsel around in his mouth — and suddenly froze.

"Master Wu is the empire's blessing!" chanted a functionary from the south, once a cruel and merciless man.

The flavor was not new. Wu tensed all over. He knew this flavor from somewhere.

"Wizard!" a voice called from the depths of the hall.

Where do I know it from? Wu asked himself. He felt a tiny cramp at the thought that he had been wrong, that he had plagiarized himself and inadvertently evoked the same flavor twice.

The noise in the hall grew. As if the crowd could not bear the burden of its astonishment, the room echoed with shouts.

It isn't possible! I used a completely new approach. And still the flavor is not new. I did not create it. It came from somewhere else.

"Genius!" the functionary shouted.

"Artist!" added Mr. Hayo.

A youthful, pliable flavor. Joyful and, in its own way, simple. Fresh like moist earth under leaves in early spring. It leapt from the dish like a sound.

Wu, the morsel still between his teeth, put all his powers on alert. Imperiously mustering every part of himself, he wracked his memory — of that moment in his mouth, at the confluence of body and soul — to yield up its secret.

"Well, you've outdone yourself, Master," the old empress said, finishing her portion first, as always. "Out-mastered the master. You've given us something unique to taste. The emperor knows."

What is it? Wu agonized. That fragile consistency. The way it bursts between my teeth, that moist crunching. Juiciness that doesn't splash like when someone upsets a glass, but squirts out of hidden vessels. And in the distance: the cold sound of hunger. A young, rapacious hunger.

The empress clapped. Everyone stood. Wu gave a start. He opened his eyes and suddenly, in a fraction of a second, a white flash of enlightenment swept over him. Hunger! He was hungry! For weeks he hadn't eaten; he had only tasted. At last he knew where he had experienced that flavor.

"Music!" someone called. Small drums sounded from the hallways. Conversations rose like water in a pool. Wu indistinctly saw movements, someone waved to him, someone bowed to him. It was precisely how wild radish tastes. He heard the word *ovation*.

Radish. Suddenly he felt it on his tongue again, the taste of long-ago fast-days.

The servants changed the candles, and for a while the hall floated in a blinding glow. Wu was no longer in doubt. Yes, he had conjured up the taste of radish. During fasts they had secretly gone to pick them. There had been a whole field of them behind the monastery. Oh, the effort! At dawn they had chewed the radishes with children's teeth. Sneaking along the narrow field path ... dozens of identically shaven little monks, indistinguishable in the morning fog. The oh so ordinary wild radish. Grubbing in the wet soil with their fingers. Oh, the effort!

Wu remembered his half-year of despair, but also the wonder of the last night, not dissimilar to the firm happiness of youth. Just then, as if the floor had begun to slide out from under him with a clang, his seventy-eight years began to disappear beneath him. All the exertion ever channeled through him from the heavens down to the earth culminated in an agonizing effort to stand up.

A dignitary from the east, whom he barely knew, quickly jumped up from his table.

"O chosen one!" he said, offering an old-fashioned bow, almost to his knees. "O Master, I search in vain for the words ... I hesitate to ... I couldn't dare to ... only my position might give me the right to ask..."

Wu did not answer. He nodded absent-mindedly, to show he was listening, but he heard nothing and groped his way to a row of pillars. His head was spinning. The drummer banged loudly on his drum. The dancing began. Radish.

Time disappearing into time, so many years of self-denial. Those years of effort, plunging into time like a knife into wet clay, had finally yielded up a flavor as simple and old as the world. This madness for the new, this obsession with uniqueness, which had cast him onto this steep path, defying everything that did not yet exist ... Wu staggered along the hallway.

"Lead the emperor away!" said the censor back in the hall, in a quiet but very sharp voice.

*

When Wu had fumbled his way down to the foot of the stairs, he heard a shout from the palace. Dimly he saw the shimmering lights cast someone's distorted shadow across the staircase. He did not care what was happening, but before he could pass through the gate, someone gently blocked his path.

"Wu," an all too familiar voice whispered carefully, "follow me. Quietly. Don't turn around."

Wu followed. It was night again, the first night in many years that he had nothing he needed to do. His mind a blank, he paced after the tall figure, strangely slender in the dark, until they reached the garden by the pond. Finally the shadow stopped amid the shadows.

"Wu," it said again, "I don't have much time. Has your nephew gone?"

Wu nodded. He stared at the black ball of branches swaying in the night breeze. Leaves rustled.

"Good. Wu, I managed to alter the charge. He's only been convicted of illegal possession, for removing materials from the emperor's library."

The night, alive with its own life, spoke in screeches.

"It's better this way. That poem ... I destroyed it. No one besides the two of us knows about it. You won't say anything about it, of course. It's a solution."

A veiled question was hidden in the censor's words, but Wu merely stared into the gray moonlight.

"Your nephew is lucky," the censor continued. "The emperor is on his deathbed. I think he will not live till morning. Tomorrow there will be confusion everywhere, and before anyone remembers, the boy will be beyond the Five Rivers."

Wu suddenly felt cold. Repetition, it occurred to him, but without the word. He hid his hands in his long sleeves. Multiplication, proliferation. Nothing can wrench from existence that which it does not contain. Although only autumn, it was nearly freezing.

"It's truly better this way," the shadow repeated with a hint of pleading in its voice, which only someone who had studied it diligently would recognize. "I know what I'm doing. Trust me."

"Yes," Wu said absently. Searching. The source, the spring of desire. And all rivers flow to the sea.

"Wu, I have to go back. Will you forgive me?" the censor asked humbly. He retreated a step. Wu nodded. The other old man suddenly placed his hand on his heart and bowed to him in a mute farewell. Wu did the same. For a moment they stood like that in the darkness, bowing to each other, and then the censor turned and quickly vanished among the cherry trees.

Wu sat down on the grass. It was already moist with morning dew. His nephew, meanwhile, was wandering along the shore of an unknown river, slipping along its muddy embankment, and because he was a person whose destiny was impatience and yearning, he sobbed loudly, breaking his nails on the icy stones. Wu sat, eyes closed, and with strict attentiveness followed the slow disappearance of time beneath his feet until morning, when the long palace trumpets informed the realm of the emperor's death.

Daniela Fischerová (b. 1948) is a leading Czech writer of the generation born after the Second World War. She is best known for her plays, which have been staged around the world, including in the United States. She is also known for her children's books, screenplays, and radio plays.

Her first play, *Dog and Wolf*, caused such a political scandal that she was banned from having her plays performed for eight years. *Dog and Wolf* and *Sudden Misfortune* have both been translated into English and performed in the U.S.

Fischerová lives in Prague with her husband and their teenage daughter.

The book's translator, **Neil Bermel** (b. 1965), teaches Czech and Russian at Sheffield University in England. He has translated two novels by the noted Czech writer Pavel Kohout: *The Widow Killer* (1998) and *I Am Snowing* (1994). A graduate of Yale University, he received his doctorate in Slavic Languages and Literatures from University of California, Berkeley. He grew up in New Rochelle, New York.

The jacket illustrations were done by **Irena Šafránková,** a Czech artist living in Prague. The book was set in Sabon and printed by Quebecor Worldwide in Fairfield, Pennsylvania. The jacket was printed by Strine Printing in York, Pennsylvania.